CLAIMING HER MATES: BOOK THREE

DIA COLE

Claiming Her Mates: Book Three

Published by Black Diamond Press LLC.

Cover Art by Addendum Designs

ISBN: 978-1-946975-23-2

For us to live, the bitch must die...

The happy-ever-after I'm seeking seems farther away than ever. Nathan refuses to accept my other mates and the secret I'm keeping may destroy any possible future between the five of us.

Even worse, Tasha's arrival puts us all in grave danger. No one takes what is hers and lives.

Our only chance for survival is to defeat the psychotic Alpha female. But how can we kill an immortal?

For my miracles...

PROLOGUE

Tyberius

T *wo weeks before Christmas...*

MY BELOVED'S CRIES SLICED THROUGH THE HOWLING NIGHT wind to pierce my heart. Cursing the oath I'd made to my brother, I contorted my six-foot-seven body to fit on the tiny concrete slab that passed as a balcony in this dump.

Havana deserved more than this run-down apartment complex. The entire two-room flat she shared with her room-mate could easily fit inside one of the luxurious bedrooms in Nathan's estate. She should be lying on silk sheets with him instead of on a threadbare futon sobbing her eyes out.

A deep yearning made me place one hand on the icy glass sliding door that stood between us. I longed to rush into her room and offer her comfort, but she belonged to my brother and I belonged to the darkness.

My ability to cloak myself in shadows made me an excellent spymaster for both my mother and brother. But, here and now, I'd trade my affinity for the dark to step into the light of Havana's bedroom.

My phone buzzed inside my back pocket.

Blast. Her again. There was no need to look at the device. I'd bet my Volante convertible it was yet another tirade from Mommy Dearest. She'd been ordering me home to Winterhaven for days. I let out a heavy sigh knowing I'd return to her, as I always did.

But first I have to make sure Havana is okay.

I studied her through the glass. Although her hip-length dark hair hid the stunning beauty of her face, the red T-shirt she wore bared her long supple legs to my hungry gaze.

I both cursed and congratulated myself for giving Havana that shirt after one of our dates.

"Ty, since you won't sleep with me, let me sleep with this." Havana had tugged on my shirt and, unable to deny her anything, I'd torn the garment off my back.

She'd slept in it nearly every night since. It made no sense, as she barely knew I existed.

She didn't remember the times we picnicked under the stars, or all the movies we'd watched together—I always let her pick those sappy romantic comedies. And she didn't remember all the hours we spent in my brother's study—her curvaceous body pressed against mine as I read to her. She'd once told me nothing soothed her like the sound of my voice.

If only I could offer her solace now.

Her slender frame shook with the force of her crying.

I curled my hands into fists, wanting to ease her suffering. Not being able to comfort her was the worst form of agony I'd ever endured. Since my mother's primary love language was torture that was saying a lot.

My bond with my brother was the only reason I'd

survived my childhood. Our ability to seek refuge in each other's minds saved my sanity when Mother locked me in the darkest corner of her dungeon for weeks, sometimes months, on end. I'd often returned the favor when Mother had beaten and starved Nathan to the point of death.

It had been the two of us against Mother for as long as I could remember. There were almost no limits to what I'd do for Nathan. I'd spy for him. I'd betray Mother for him. Except for my darkest secret, I'd shared everything with him including my sexual conquests so he could briefly remember what passion felt like before Mother shackled him in silver.

But I'd initially refused to date Havana for him.

I, Tyberius Digoski, did not date. *Hell no.* And not just because females had been throwing themselves at me since adolescence. No. I did not date because to show more than a passing interest in any female put a target on their head. Mother would gladly use anyone I cared for as leverage over me and then she'd kill them anyway just for spite. No one, except my niece and brother, were exempt from Mother's murderous machinations.

But Nathan insisted I date Havana. So I did and promptly fell under her spell. *A more beautiful, intelligent, sensitive female never walked this earth.*

I rubbed the gold hoop earring I wore in my left earlobe. It was one of hers that she'd lost during a late night poetry reading. I'd torn apart Nathan's study to find it, but when I tried to return it, she'd pressed it into my palm. *"Keep it, so you'll always remember me, Sugar Bear."*

It was the greatest of ironies that she'd never remember me. Nathan had insisted I wipe her mind after every one of our dates, and then he'd made me promise to never use compulsion on her. Since I now couldn't compel her to remember me, she never would.

As my favorite poet, Byron once wrote, '*In secret we met—in silence I grieve, that thy heart could forget, thy spirit deceive.*'

I was nothing to her. Nothing.

That was abundantly clear months ago when Nathan begged me to make love to Havana for him. Finally being able to touch what my body craved more than breath had shaken my soul, but it had done nothing for her.

Havana's slumberous dark eyes had never left Nathan's face.

She remembered him, not me. She wanted him, not me.

It'd cost me everything to push my brother at her and walk away, but that's what I'd done. I'd hoped their happiness would make up for my pain and it had.

Until three months ago when Mother had shown up with her Enforcers, and her knives, and her bloodlust. Nathan had been forced to end things with Havana to save her from certain death. To say it devastated Havana was an understatement.

She'd initially refused to leave her room or eat. Just when I thought she'd need hospitalization, her roommate had finally bullied her into rejoining the outside world.

Over time, Havana's crying spells had grown less frequent and I'd hoped she'd recovered.

As if someone can recover from losing their true love. I glanced around the side of the apartment, hoping to see the roommate's light. *Perhaps Sydney can intervene?* Then I remembered she worked late tonight. Havana was alone.

The sound of my beloved's sadness carried through the glass.

I tensed holding back the primal need to go to my mate. *No. She's Nathan's mate.*

Havana sniffed loudly and reached for a bottle of pills on her nightstand.

Pills? A coldness settled over me as Havana spilled the medication into her palm.

Fuck no. Before I could even consider the ramifications, I yanked open the balcony door and strode into her room. "Stop."

Havana jumped to her feet with a pain-filled gasp. The pill bottle fell from her hand and small white pills scattered in all directions. "What the hell?" She blinked as if trying to place me. "Tyberius? What are you doing here?"

"I won't allow you to kill yourself," I said, motioning at the pill bottle still rocking back and forth on the scratched laminate floor.

"I'm taking the pills for a back injury. I fell on some stairs at work." She rubbed the small of her back.

"Oh." I felt like a fool.

Her eyes narrowed and filled with suspicion. "Are you watching me?"

"I'll go now." I turned toward the balcony.

"Oh, no you don't." She darted in front of me, blocking my escape. It was impossible not to notice the outline of her pointed nipples against the soft thin fabric of my shirt. That damn shirt left so much of her golden skin on display—her toned thighs, the curves of her calves, her gorgeous bare feet.

Even from across the room, her intoxicating floral scent filled my nostrils. It was muskier than before and filled with pheromones that made me burn for her.

Realization jolted me. *She's close to her first transition.* Every Lykos male in a ten-mile radius would come for her. *Nathan needs to know.* We could no longer keep her origins a secret. "I must leave."

Havana boldly held my gaze. "Not until you explain yourself."

Blast. Nathan would have my ass for this. Havana wasn't supposed to know I was keeping tabs on her. Since compelling her to forget me was out of the question, I was well and truly fucked. *How am I getting out of this one?*

"I've had my fill of stalkers." She grabbed her phone from her nightstand and held it in her hand. "You have two seconds to tell me why you're here before I call the cops."

Damn it to hell. Involving the human police would make this even messier than it was. Seeing no choice, I caught her gaze and said, "Remember me."

Havana let out a cry, dropped her phone, and clutched her head in her hands.

I hated that the compulsion caused her pain, but it was temporary.

A moment later, Havana blinked and looked up at me. "Ty!" Then she launched herself at me. "I've missed you, Sugar Bear."

I caught her as I always did and, even though it was forbidden and wrong, I embraced her.

This is the last time I'll ever hold her like this.

Her scent—night blooming jasmine—surrounded me and filled my mind with the images of the last time we'd held each other. She'd taken me in her mouth... Fuck that had been incredible.

My cock kicked eagerly against my fly.

Havana pulled away, her deep brown eyes dancing with mirth. "Do you have something in your pocket or are you happy to see me?"

Gaining some semblance of self-control, I stepped away. "I'm always happy to see you."

"Then why haven't you come see me? It's been so long." Tears shimmered in her eyes.

She's crying? For me? "Things have been busy." That wasn't a lie. The most recent attempt on Mother's life had destroyed her twisted dream and taken the tiny bit of sanity she'd possessed. Mother had been torturing, killing, and declaring wars on other factions right and left.

Havana chewed her plump lower lip. "I thought it was because of what happened with Nathan." She frowned as if struggling to recall something. "You and I were finally getting together and then he was there. Why was he there?"

I went motionless. We didn't know exactly how the mind compulsion affected her long-term memories. Apparently, it made her recall the threesome with Nathan in a different light.

"Why would I have sex with Nathan? You're the one I love, Ty."

"You love me?" My heart rejoiced even as I knew it couldn't last. She would forget me when I left.

She looked at me through her thick lashes. "I do."

"And I love you, Starfire," I confessed.

Her glorious smile lit up the room. "So you're not mad at me."

"On the contrary." I was the lowest bastard for reaching out and hauling her back into my arms.

She let out a small whimper that had me setting her down and inspecting her perfect body. "Show me where it hurts?"

"It's nothing," she said with a dismissive wave. Then a mischievous light sparked in those dark chocolate eyes of hers. "Actually, I'm in a lot of pain." She kicked the balcony door shut and drew the curtains. "So much pain." Giving me a seductive smile that melted my bones, she drew the shirt over her head and tossed it on the floor. She was naked.

My brain blanked at the sight of her silky smooth skin, large firm breasts topped by dusky rose-colored nipples, and the small strip of hair covering her sex.

"Your body is exquisite in every way," I murmured.

She took my hand and placed it on the small of her back. "It hurts here."

The contrast between the much darker hue of my skin and hers captivated me.

"And it hurts here." She moved my hand between her legs.

I couldn't help slipping a finger inside her. She was hot, wet, and tight.

"Oh, yes," Havana cried. She undulated against my hand all the while tearing at my clothes.

I only realized she'd opened my pants, when her soft, warm hand wrapped around my cock.

Fuuuck. I nearly fell over. "You can't."

"We can." She worked her palm up and down over me in a rhythm that nearly blinded me with lust.

"I need you, Ty," she moaned. "Please don't push me away this time."

As if I could. All these months without her had left me starving for her touch. I needed her. And she needed me.

Just this once.

As if driven by madness, I picked her up and carried her to her shabby dresser.

One swipe of my hand sent her hairbrush and styling products careening to the floor. Then I set her down and kissed her deeply.

Her tongue and lips danced with mine, while our hands roamed each other's bodies.

Needing to taste her, I dipped my mouth to her nipples and took one and then the other into my mouth.

Her pleasured moans fueled the fire in my blood.

More. Give her more pleasure.

I leaned her back against the dresser mirror, pushed her legs onto my shoulders, and brought my lips to her center.

She let out a wild cry. "Yes. Oh, yes." She tasted of the richest ambrosia—musty and sweet.

I couldn't get enough of her honey, but all too soon she was thrashing against my tongue begging me for release.

I sucked hard on her pearl and she came apart, trembling and crying my name.

It was fucking incredible.

"More," she begged, grabbing hold of my collar and dragging me to my feet. She shoved down my pants and wrapped her legs around my waist.

The brush of her wet heat against my cock made my hands shake.

Need this. Need her.

Some part of my mind screamed at me to stop. *She's Nathan's.*

"No." I tried to step away, but she locked her ankles together.

"Don't push me away. Please." She rubbed me against her.

I inhaled deeply, trying to suck in enough oxygen to fire up my willpower.

Her seductive scent infiltrated my nostrils, stripping me of all self-restraint. With one thrust of my hips, I buried myself in my brother's mate.

"Ty," she cried, arching off the dresser.

Her searing wet heat milked me as our bodies came together in a hard, desperate mating that rocked the dresser back and forth.

The mirror crashed to the floor, splintering into a million pieces.

Fuck the mirror.

She came again and again. Her body clamping down on me.

I followed her over the abyss crying her name.

She clung to me, kissing my chest, my neck, and my face.

I branded each one of those intimate touches to memory. Never would I forget this. I slowly withdrew from her body and carried her to the futon.

She gave me a sleepy smile as I drew her covers over her. "Stay with me tonight."

If only I could. I kissed her lips one last time and then held her gaze. "Go to sleep, Starfire. And forget me."

Her eyes fluttered closed and her breathing deepened.

As I fastened my pants, I waited for the blistering guilt to hit. But it never did. *She's my mate too,* a voice whispered in my mind. *But I can't have her. Never again.*

As Byron said, 'If I should meet thee after long years, how should I greet thee? With silence and tears.' With my head hung low, I retreated to the shadows and let the darkness consume me.

❧ 1 ☙

HAVANA

C hristmas Day...

THE DECORATIONS ON THE SKI RESORT CHRISTMAS TREE shook as three children gleefully tore through colorfully wrapped gifts beneath its boughs. Their laughter filled me with joy.

Sinking into the warm embrace of my armchair, I inhaled the wintery aroma of the garland strung around picture windows overlooking silvery banks of snow. The fragrance mixed wonderfully with the smoky scent of the fire crackling in the rustic fireplace.

It all was so damn near perfect I could almost ignore the bloodstains on the carpet, the lingering odor of rot in the air, and the gnawing feeling that something terrible was going to happen.

Taking a deep breath, I tried to stomp out the irrational anxiety. We'd all survived our hellish encounters with the dead yesterday and I wasn't going to let anything ruin the celebration. I'd been dreaming about having a real Christmas with decorations, presents, and a family my entire life. The closest I'd ever come to it as a lonely child had been the television specials I'd watched from my mom's dirty trailer floor. This was so much better than a scripted show.

Over by the Christmas tree, the Ackerman boys and Mira, the daughter of my newest mate, let out ecstatic cries as they tore through the wrapped gifts like pint-sized tornados.

I couldn't help but laugh at their excitement.

I wasn't alone. Several of the human survivors milling around the snack table cracked a smile too. Seeing the terror and shock slowly leave their eyes warmed my heart. Those poor people had been through so much watching their friends and family members die. *They don't need to be frightened any longer.* I sat up straighter in my chair. With my new abilities, I could protect them from the dead.

But can I protect them from what's coming? Doubt heightened my feeling of unease.

Trying to shake off the premonition, I focused instead on the gorgeous, muscular males surrounding my armchair. All four of my mates were anxious over my dizzy spell a few moments ago, but they didn't need to worry. There was a good reason for my vertigo. I gently laid my palm over my abdomen trying to sense the spark of new life growing inside me.

We're going to have a baby! My chest tightened with happiness and excitement. All my life I'd wanted to have a big family. I just never figured on my children having so many daddies. I bit my lower lip to muffle my giggle. Soon, I'd have to spill my secret to my mates, but not now. Now I just wanted to enjoy our first holiday together.

A soft sound drew my attention to Liam, my seven-foot-tall auburn haired teddy bear of a mate who sat in the armchair across from mine. The nine-month-old infant he cradled against his bare chest sucked on his right knuckle as he hummed her a lullaby.

"You're great with Sierra," I said with a smile. *He'll be an awesome father.*

Liam stroked his hand through the baby's silky tuff of dark hair. "She's a pretty babe, isn't she?"

I nodded. "She's precious. I'm so glad she's okay."

"Me too." Liam met my gaze and we shared the horrible memory of the helicopter crash yesterday. It was a miracle everyone survived.

A loud shriek drew my attention back to the tree. Sierra's oldest brother, Kaden, was holding a stuffed bear over the head of three-year-old Jackson.

Mira tried to grab the bear from Kaden. "Give it back to him."

Kaden shook his head. "He's trying to eat the hat."

Despite the older boy being considerably taller than her, Mira put her hands on her hips and stared into his eyes. "Give Jackson his bear!" Even from over here, I heard the other-worldly ring in her tone.

Kaden's expression went slack and he immediately dropped the stuffed toy into his brother's outreached hands.

Ah, hell. Mira was using compulsion. Again.

"Good." Mira threw back her silver-streaked hair. "And give me your candy cane."

Without so much as blinking, the older boy reached for his candy.

Shaking my head, I looked over at Nathan to see if he was watching his daughter break the rules.

The Alpha male stood nose to nose with Gabriel, my most aggressive mate, oblivious to anything but their tele-pathic argument.

Seeing that he'd be no help, I mentally chided Mira. *"Stop compelling Kaden this instant."*

The headstrong little girl jerked her head in my direction, a surprised look on her face. *"You're talking to me like Daddy does."*

I didn't know that Nathan spoke with her telepathically. I wondered what else the little girl knew of our species. *"Should we tell him you're using compulsion?"* I pretended to look for Nathan behind my chair.

Her eyes rounded and she shook her head. *"I'm sorry. I'll stop."*

"Why don't you unwrap more presents?" I suggested.

"Okay." She grabbed the closest gift, tore off the wrapping paper, and held up a bottle of champagne. "Look, Vana! I got some juice."

I coughed. "That's great, love bug." Maybe tossing in the random gifts I'd found in the luggage behind the front desk hadn't been the best idea. *God only knows what else the kids might find.*

The handsome blond doctor sitting in the armchair next to mine called out, "Let me see that juice, Miss Mira. It may have medicinal properties." He stood and wiped away an imaginary wrinkle on his slacks. Only Mason would manage to scrounge up a pair of clean pants and a collared shirt. While he looked as dignified as ever, the rest of us looked like half-dressed hobos.

Mira glared at Mason. "No. It's mine." She clutched the bottle tightly to her chest and pouted like only a four-year-old could.

"Bollocks. That's a 1959 Dom Perignon." Mason's telepathic voice carried his sexy British accent.

I laughed. *"Don't worry. She'll forget about it if you offer her that."* I nodded in the direction of a royal blue velvet box I'd set on a side table. The box contained an antique diamond butterfly hairpin I knew Mira would love.

"What if she refuses?"

"She won't." No female of any age could resist diamonds that size. As if on their own accord, my fingers slid into the front pocket of the white terry-cloth robe I wore. The stunning engagement ring Nathan gave me a few hours ago was still there. I absently rubbed the four-carat princess cut diamond still shocked at discovering Nathan had planned on proposing to me instead of breaking up with me that terrible night all those months ago.

I wished I could take back the river of tears I'd cried over him since that night. Even though I now knew the truth—he'd broken up with me to save me from his ex—the memory of the pain he'd put me through still stung.

Mason kissed my cheek. *"All right, here goes nothing."* He strode over to the table, picked up the velvet box, and then walked over to Mira.

The little girl turned and smiled at the doctor. Her amber eyes, so like Nathan's, brightened.

I twisted my head around, hoping her father was watching the exchange.

Nathan and Gabriel growled at each other. Evenly matched in their six-foot-four height, they both possessed the muscular build of NFL linemen and they both were barely dressed. I hummed my approval as the flannel blanket knotted around Nathan's waist dipped low enough to show the taut muscles of his six-pack.

I licked my lips hoping the blanket might slip further. From our steamy encounter in this very chair, I knew Nathan wore nothing under it. My skin warmed and my nipples hardened in memory of our makeup sex. I could definitely go for more of that right now.

"You're mistaken, Ambassador. Havana is mated to us all."

Gabriel flexed one of his huge biceps drawing my gaze to his gorgeous bronze skin. The dark-haired male wore only a pair of jeans so tattered I could clearly see his muscular thighs. My breathing quickened as I remembered Gabriel using those powerful muscles to pound into me at the resort pool just a little while ago.

"Not for long." Nathan chuckled. "I've asked Vana to choose between us. Who do you think she'll pick? Three males that were strangers two weeks ago or the male whose engagement ring she carries in her pocket?"

And just like that my bubble of happiness popped and a pit formed in my stomach.

Nathan continued. "You'll understand if I don't invite you to our wedding, Enforcer."

Gabriel snarled.

Crap. I clenched Nathan's engagement ring so tightly it dug into the palm of my hand. *Why can't he accept my other mates?* There had to be some way of convincing Nathan to give the five of us a chance. *We can work. I know it.*

Liam looked over at me. *"Ignore them, Beautiful. Focus on the kids. They're having a good time, aren't they?"*

He's right. I won't let Nathan and Gabriel ruin this. I dropped the engagement ring back into my pocket and looked over at Mira.

The little girl danced around the tree clutching her new butterfly hairpin.

Mason raised the bottle of champagne in my direction. *"It worked."*

I started to congratulate him, but soft footsteps stole my attention.

Rebecca, a middle-aged woman with greying hair and deep laugh lines around her mouth, approached. "I can take my granddaughter now." She held her arms outstretched to Liam. To her credit her hands only shook slightly. I gave the older woman props. Few would try to take anything from a male Liam's size. My respect for the woman, who'd apparently been the principal of an elementary school, grew.

Liam hesitated for a split second and then gently transitioned the sleeping baby to Rebecca.

Cradling Sierra against her chest with practiced ease, Rebecca turned her attention to me. "Are we moving to another location?"

I nodded. "We're going to caravan up the mountain to Sanctuary. The lodge there has enough supplies for everyone." There was no safer place for us all to ride out the apocalypse. Sanctuary had running water and electricity along with enough food and supplies to last us for years. Thank God, Nathan had ordered Liam, Mason, and Gabriel to bring me there ten days ago. If they hadn't... I shivered imagining what might have happened.

Rebecca gazed at the tightly clustered group of survivors. "Marshall has convinced some of the others that we should stay."

I glanced at the thin, balding man gesturing wildly to the others. Marshall had been someone important—a company vice president, CEO, or some crap like that. It didn't matter. He along with everyone else would need to stick with my crew if they wanted to survive.

Liam stood, the top of his head nearly scraping the slanted wood beam ceiling. "Tell Marshall, he does what Havana says or he'll die."

Rebecca took a step back.

Although my mate needed to work on his delivery, I appreciated him having my back. "What Liam means is that it will be safer for everyone at Sanctuary." At some point, any zombies in the nearby town would head here in search for living prey. *Is that the threat I sense?*

Rebecca nodded. "I'll talk to them." She marched over to

the group of survivors. Within minutes the humans were arguing.

Humans. Crap. Listen to me. When did I start thinking that way?

Over by the tree, Mira was trying to yank the champagne bottle out of Mason's hands. "Give me my juice."

"Miss Mira, we made a trade fair and square. Your juice for the diamond heirloom."

The little girl stamped her foot. "No!"

Mason sent me a helpless look.

Time for her dad to get involved. I turned my head. "Nathan can you..."

Mira's father shoved Gabriel. "I'll pound you into dust, Enforcer."

Gabriel bared his teeth and pushed Nathan back. "Do you really want another ass kicking, Ambassador?"

Both of the males' hair stood on end and their eyes sparked with aggression.

Goddamn it. They were going to fight. Again.

As my annoyance rose, I pinched the bridge of my nose wondering if I should make good on my threat to compel the two to be friends.

"Let's take this outside," growled Nathan.

Irritation morphed into worry as I watched the two males stalk outside. *I have to stop them.*

As I pushed myself to my feet, Liam dragged me into his lap. "Let them work it out."

"Nathan might not survive another encounter." The Alpha male had been pretty messed up from his fight with Gabriel just a few hours earlier and that was on top of him nearly dying yesterday.

Liam snorted. "Don't worry. Gabriel knows Nathan is mated to you and if one of your mates dies, we all die. He won't risk your life."

Liam's words eased some of my anxiety.

"But they're ruining Christmas." I hated that my eyes filled with tears. *Damn hormones.* "All I wanted was for all of us to have a real freaking holiday experience." *Is that too much to ask?*

"This is the real holiday experience." Liam gave me a wry grin. "At least all of mine were like this. Children screaming. Males fighting."

"Really?"

He chuckled. "Usually my mom threw me and my brothers outside before we could destroy her furniture."

I blinked trying to picture a family of giants. "Were all your brothers as large as you?"

"No." His smile faded. "My mother always said I was a freak of nature." His shame and embarrassment leaked through our bond.

How could any mother say that to their child, much less to Liam? He was the sweetest guy ever. I wrapped my arms around his waist and hugged him. "You're not a freak, you're perfect and I'm so glad you're mine."

Liam gave me a swoon worthy smile and whispered in my ear, "Do you think we could have that alone time now?" He telepathically replayed our earlier conversation where I'd promised him some one-on-one time in the pool.

"Right now?" I glanced out the window seeing nothing but fluffy white snow. Gabriel and Nathan must have taken their fight away from the resort.

Across the room, Mason pleaded with Mira while the Ackerman boys ran in circles around them shrieking loudly.

The racket had woken Sierra who screeched like a dying peacock.

Rebecca tried to shush the baby back to sleep while Marshall shouted, "It's suicide to leave. We have everything we need."

"But Nathan said we should go to Sanctuary," another survivor cried.

Marshall narrowed his watery eyes. "Screw Nathan."

"Nathan should have let the zombies eat that guy," Liam muttered. "Come on, let's get out of here."

I sighed and rubbed my temples. This definitely was not the Christmas of my dreams. "As tempting as your offer is, I need to fix this." *First I'll deal with Gabriel and Nathan and then I'll set the humans straight.*

Liam cupped my face in his hands. "This will all be here in an hour. Escape with me for a little while. Let me worship you."

"Worship?"

He nodded eagerly. "From the top of your head to your beautiful toes."

Heat curled between my thighs. That sounded pretty amazing. I looked over the chaotic lobby. *I'll bet no one will notice if we skip out for a bit.* "Lead the way, big guy."

He grinned from ear to ear and dragged me down the hallway.

‽ 2 ‽

HAVANA

Despite his large size, Liam walked softly and not a single person turned their head when we ducked down the hallway and pushed through a door near the elevators.

We stopped inside the pitch-black room.

The bleachy smell of chlorine and the lingering scent of the passion I'd shared with Gabriel filled the air. The erotic memories of my time with the dark-haired male made my nipples pebble against the terry cloth fabric of my robe.

Liam whirled around, hauled me into his arms, and kissed me. He tasted of candy canes and chocolate, an intoxicating flavor I couldn't get enough of.

Kicking off my flip-flops, I wrapped my legs around his waist and pressed myself flush against him.

Our lips and tongues slow danced and then, as if some inaudible song had quickened its beat, our kiss deepened. Desire, hot and sweet, drugged my mind.

He kneaded my ass, while I caressed his broad shoulders and ripped biceps. His body was a thing of beauty and I wanted to savor every inch especially the impressive bulge pressing insistently against the fly of his jeans.

Moaning, I sucked his tongue into my mouth and rocked my hips against him.

"Havana," Liam panted. He tried to slip his hand under my robe, but I'd belted it tightly. He cursed under his breath and tugged the fabric apart.

The light tinkling sound of metal hitting the pool deck made me break our kiss and look down.

Nathan's engagement ring lay next to Liam's right foot.

Crap. It must have fallen out of my pocket.

Liam tensed, his expression falling. "So Nathan was telling the truth. He asked you to marry him?"

I sighed. "He did."

"Will you?"

I paused, not having really considered it until now. The five of us were already soul bonded, did we really need the pomp and circumstance of a wedding? But then again, the idea of a romantic ceremony where we cemented our love for each other had a lot of appeal. "I'd like to marry him at the same time I marry you, Mason, and Gabriel." What a wedding that would be. Syd, my best friend, and I had fanta-sized about our weddings together. She'd flip her lid if she knew mine would involve more than one groom. *Ah, hell.* I hoped she was safe somewhere.

Liam let out a deep breath. "You'd marry me?" Our bond thrummed with his relief and happiness.

"Hell, yes." I rose on the balls of my feet to kiss him.

He stared down at my lips. "But Nathan won't go for that. He wants you to choose."

"Fuck choosing." I grabbed the back of his head and forced his lips to meet mine. I wasn't giving up any of my mates.

The kiss quickly turned toe-curling hot. I thought for sure

he'd rip off my robe and take me against the door. Instead, he pulled away and scanned the room. "Jacuzzi or the pool?" His werewolf vision, like mine, allowed him to see both the lap-pool and the Jacuzzi perfectly in the dark.

Although both options were fine, I felt drawn to the hot tub. "How about the Jacuzzi?" The water would be cold and the jets wouldn't work without electricity, but we could sit down in there—or rather, I could sit on Liam in there. My heart pounded while my dirty mind raced with possibilities. The tub was even big enough to accommodate all my mates if they joined us.

All my mates...

The idea of all four males in the water... kissing me... touching me.... loving me... made heat move low in my body. *Of course, Nathan and Gabriel have to stop punching each other long enough to pay attention to me. Bastards.*

"Jacuzzi it is." Liam tugged me through the maze of lounge chairs and tables until we got to the hot tub. Then he stopped at the edge and dipped his bare foot into the water. He frowned. "The water is cold."

"I'm sure we could heat it up," I said, winking.

Lust sparked through our connection. He turned toward me and reached for the belt of my robe.

Not so fast. Despite having sex multiple times, Liam and I had never been together alone. The other guys had always been there. I wanted this time to be special for my former virgin. I brushed his hands away and smiled coyly. "Sit down for a minute." I gestured at the nearby lounge chair.

His brows knit together. "You don't want me to take off your robe?"

"No." Before his expression could fall, I added, "I want to take it off for you." I didn't have many marketable skills, but I sure as hell knew how to undress in front of a guy. "Sit down and I'll give you a show."

Liam's eyes widened and he licked his lips. "Okay." Never taking his eyes from me, he dropped back onto the lounge chair.

With a loud snapping sound, the vinyl straps broke and Liam fell straight through to the floor.

Oh, no! "Liam! Are you okay?"

He sat up, his face reddening. "Yeah, guess these things aren't meant for males my size."

I felt terrible as he pushed himself out of the destroyed chair and shoved it across the pool deck. "I'm sorry. I didn't think—"

"Don't apologize," he said interrupting me. "That kind of thing has been happening all my life. Freak of nature, remember?"

My heart tripped over itself. I couldn't believe this gorgeous, magnificent male thought so poorly of himself. If I ever met his mother, I'd kick her in the crotch. "You're no freak of nature and I never want to hear you say that again." I needed to show him how much I appreciated him, supersize and all.

"Yes, my Alpha," he said, with a much more genuine smile.

I tossed my hair back. "I've changed my mind about the chair. You stand right there."

He froze as if I'd compelled him not to move.

"Relax, big guy. We're going to have some fun." I circled my mate, admiring his incredibly broad chest. I traced my hands across it, loving the soft springy auburn chest hair so different from my other mates. "You have bigger guns than anyone I've ever seen." I caressed his shredded biceps, thinking of the body builder I'd dated years ago. That guy had won the Southwest Body Building Championship and his body didn't hold a candle to Liam's ripped physique.

Liam growled softly under his breath. "I'll kill him whoever he is."

I laughed realizing he must've been picking up on my thoughts. "That guy's a loser and I haven't seen him in years." Given the state of the world these days, I'd likely never see him again. "Besides, he didn't have muscles like this." I ran my hand down his stomach, loving the way his rock hard abs danced.

Liam sucked in a breath as I unbuttoned his fly and released his massive cock.

An erotic thrill shot through me as it swelled and throbbed in my hands. His shaft was a thing of beauty, as long as my forearm and as thick as his wrists. I couldn't even wrap my fingers fully around it. I wet my lips thinking of how no male had ever filled me the way Liam had. A hungry ache stirred between my thighs.

A strange half growl-half purring sound filled the air.

Liam's gaze flew to my lips and I realized the noise was coming from me.

Getting a grip on my lust before I tackled him to the floor, I stepped away. "Take off your pants."

Liam quickly kicked off his jeans, the fabric landing on the pieces of the broken chair.

"Now go wait for me in the Jacuzzi."

My mate quickly stepped into the tub and obediently sat down. The cold seemed to have no effect on his cock as the smooth, pink crown breached the surface of the water. "What else do you want, my Alpha?"

Good question. I smiled. Although I enjoyed being dominated during sex, being in control came naturally to me. *Hell.* I'd played a dominatrix on stage for years. After being so thoroughly worked over by Gabriel earlier, I needed to feel more in control of my body. Also, I sensed Liam would enjoy a little power play. "Now I want you to watch."

I slowly undid my belt, keeping my robe from gaping open. Then, I danced seductively for him revealing an inch of my skin at a time.

Liam's breathing grew labored—our bond simmering with lust.

Wanting to rock his world, I threw off the robe and cupped my breasts in my hands.

He inhaled sharply when I pinched my nipples.

"Do you enjoy watching me?" I slid one leg up on the Jacuzzi handrail. The position exposed my sex to his hungry gaze.

"Fuck yeah," he gasped, rising out of the water. Impossibly his massive cock had grown even larger.

"I'll touch mine if you touch yours." I caressed the hard points of my nipples, loving the way his pupils dilated. Then I slid my hand between my legs, careful to keep my balance.

Liam groaned and wrapped his fist around himself.

"That's it. I want to see you touch yourself." I rubbed teasing circles around my clit.

He moaned my name and ran his fist from crown to root.

"Faster," I ordered, loving the way he bit down on his lower lip.

He complied, thrusting his hips in time to the rhythm of his hand.

Watching him pleasure himself cranked my desire even higher. My core ached with wanting, growing wetter and wetter. "I can't wait until I have you inside me."

His hand moved so fast over his hard flesh it was a blur.

"That's it, baby. I'm going to fuck you so hard, just like this." I inserted two fingers inside my wet channel and rocked against them.

He made a choking sound, his pupils dilating to the point his eyes were nearly all black.

Then moving impossibly fast for a man his size, he

reached up and dragged me off the rail. Using enviable strength, he held me by my hips just over the icy water. My core was pressed right against the tip of his engorged cock.

God, this is going to feel so good. I had two seconds to savor the feeling of his throbbing erection poised right where I needed it. Then, with one punch of his hips, he was sliding inside me, claiming my pussy. I cried wildly at the erotic invasion that kept going and going. My aching flesh stretched wide to take him.

Liam, showing impressive restraint, stopped short of fully impaling me.

I didn't know if it was possible to take him completely, but I wanted to try. I ground myself on his cock, working more of him inside me. I couldn't take him deep enough.

His grip on my hips tightened and he held me in place. "I don't want to hurt you."

"You won't." I pushed down on him.

"No." His eyes glowed bright green in the darkness. His raging lust poured through our bond. Somehow he kept himself in check.

I didn't want that though. I wanted him to ravage my body and fuck the worry out of me. "Give me what I need."

Bowing his head, Liam let out a ragged moan. Then he was lifting me up and down on his cock, slowly at first, then faster and faster.

Mindless with lust, I wrapped my arms around the strong column of his neck.

He bent his head and lashed his hot tongue over my nipple.

I moaned, arching my back to give him better access to my breasts. They swelled and ached for his touch.

He suckled one nipple into his mouth and then the other, all the while his strong warm hands drove me up and down on his shaft.

Cold water splashed over us, but I felt nothing but the drag of his massive dick straight over my G-spot. Pleasure coiled deep in my belly. My teeth rattled as he pistoned his hips faster.

Oh, God. Losing my grip on his shoulders, I fell back. My head hit the water, but I didn't care.

Liam shifted one hand to the middle of my back to anchor me.

So good. So fucking good. My wet hair spilled around us as I pumped my hips to the crazy fast beat of his. White light burst across my vision.

"I'm close," he gasped.

Wild pleading sounds ripped from my lips. *Right there. Oh, God. I'm right there.*

He shifted me so he could slide his hand between my legs.

One brush of his fingers over my clit and a violent orgasm exploded through me. Screaming, I rode the waves of ecstasy straight to the stars.

He rolled his hips once, twice and then came with a thunderous roar.

Chests heaving, we clung to each other. Our bond filled with bliss, contentment, and overwhelming love.

"I wish we could stay like this forever."

He murmured his agreement against my wet hair.

The sound of a door banging against the wall dragged our heads around.

Mason rushed into the room. "Stop! You can't have sex!"

3

LIAM

Doc raced over as if the Beast of Winterhaven was fast on his heels. He stopped at the edge of the Jacuzzi and stared accusingly down at me. "No one can mate with Havana in her condition."

Annoyance burned away my afterglow. I gently set Havana down on the Jacuzzi seat. When she was settled, I turned and gave Doc the look I usually reserved for the Lykos I was about to kill. "Why are you here, Omega?" I hadn't forgiven Doc for encouraging Havana to claim Nathan as her mate. Adding the Alpha male to our existing bonds had opened a shitcan of complications we could have done without.

"To stop you from mating with Havana. She's pregnant."

Not this again. I slung my arm around my mate. "No, she's not. She has a DUI."

Havana giggled. "Not quite, big guy." She kissed the side of my cheek. "It's called an IUD."

"Whatever." The human device kept her from conceiving. Although Lykos babes were an incredible blessing, I didn't mind waiting for a while. Especially when it meant we could do much more mating. I leaned over and sealed my mouth over Havana's.

Her laugher against my lips sounded like music.

I flicked my tongue against hers the way I'd seen Gabe do. I was rewarded with her breathy gasp.

Although my hands still shook from the power of the orgasm I'd just had, my cock turned to stone. I dragged her into my lap.

Her gorgeous tits bobbed on the top of the water, begging me to suckle the hard points of her nipples.

"Again?" she asked breathlessly. She looked like a water nymph I'd seen once in a painting. Breathtaking. Beautiful. Mine.

Fuck yeah, again. I caressed her nipples. "The first time was just a warm-up. This time I'm going to make good on that promise to worship you and—"

Doc knelt down and stuck a thin piece of plastic in our faces. "I was looking for a bandage in my bag when I found this."

Havana stiffened.

I grabbed the white, wand-looking thing. At the end of it was a small rectangular opening with two dark pink parallel lines on it. "What is this?"

"It's nothing." Havana plucked the plastic stick out of my hand and set it on the edge of the Jacuzzi. "Why did you need a bandage, Mason? Was someone hurt?"

Doc pursed his lips. "Jackson got a paper cut opening a present, but by the time I got the bandage, the cut had healed."

Havana's eyebrows rose. "How is that possible? Is he Lykos too?"

Doc and I shook our heads at the same time. None of the survivors, save Mira and Nathan, carried the scent of our species.

"Definitely not, but given this healing ability, I don't think the Ackerman children are entirely human either," Doc said slowly. "It might explain why their parents reanimated into more evolved... creatures."

I blinked, thinking of the vicious predators that had nearly ended our lives yesterday. They'd been evolved creatures all right. Unlike normal zombies, they'd been smart, they'd hunted in a pack, and they'd immediately healed any injuries. I'd never encountered anything like them before.

Havana's forehead wrinkled as if she were mulling something over. "If the kids could heal from small injuries like a paper cut, could they also come back from the dead?"

The memory of holding little Sierra's limp body after the chopper crash flashed into my mind. The tiny babe had been cold and lifeless. Even though I'd seen and dealt out enough death in my life to fill a human graveyard, I'd taken her loss especially hard. Then, while I was carrying the children to safety, she'd taken a breath and let out a warbling cry. I'd thought it was a fucking miracle, but maybe it was something else. Troubled, I looked over at Doc.

His golden brows drew together. "If you'd asked me a few weeks ago, I would have told you the idea was absurd. However, at this point, I won't rule anything out."

I scratched my beard trying to puzzle it out. "So some humans reanimate into zombies, others reanimate into super zombies, and others don't die at all?"

"I don't know." Doc rocked back on his heels. "Tasha had me running blood tests on all patients at Saguaro Valley General for years." He looked over at Havana. "She wanted to identify any latents in her territory."

Havana swallowed hard. "Well, good thing I never made it to the hospital then."

That was a very good thing. Who knows what Tasha would have done to Havana if she'd identified her as one of our kind? She might have killed her or forced her to join our faction. Either way, I never would have had the chance to become her mate. I clasped Havana even tighter.

Doc continued, "A small, but still significant number of the blood samples I tested were slightly abnormal. I'd assumed it was merely due to small mutations or genetic variance in the population, but now I wonder..." He tapped his chin thoughtfully. "I'll need to run tests on the Ackerman children." His gaze went to the plastic stick. "Speaking of tests, is that yours, Havana?"

"Yes," she said in a small voice.

"Why didn't you say anything?"

I looked from his accusatory expression to her guilty one. "That's a pregnancy test, isn't it?" Although I wasn't the smartest male in the room, I'd seen enough human movies to make an educated guess.

Havana licked her lips nervously. "Yeah. I was going to tell you all later when we got back to Sanctuary."

I sucked in a breath. "You're pregnant?"

She caught her lower lip between her teeth like she did when she was nervous and nodded.

I'm going to be a father? Struck dumb, I stared at her like a jackass. It didn't matter if the babe was biologically mine or not, as far as I was concerned any babe of Havana's was mine to protect and look after. Unlike my nieces and nephews who'd been taught to fear the very sight of me, this babe would grow up caring for me. My chest expanded with emotion. *I'm going to be a father!* I locked my arms around my mate and hugged her tight.

Havana let out a squeak and slapped my shoulders. "Liam! I need to breathe!"

"Sorry!" I quickly released her. Although Havana could normally toss my giant ass across the room without breaking a sweat, I'd have to watch my strength around her in her delicate state.

She smiled up at me. "So... I take it you're happy?"

I answered her question with another kiss.

She kissed me back with such passion, I forgot all about Doc being there and moved her over my aching shaft. I had to be inside her.

Doc smacked the back of my head. "You can't mate her right now."

"Ah, fuck. We've already mated." Blood drained from my face. I'd taken her hard and rough without care for anything other than chasing our pleasure. I ran my hands over Havana's stomach. "Are you okay?"

"Mmm-hmm." She nibbled my lower lip and started to sink down on my shaft.

I quickly lifted her off me. As much as I craved her body, we couldn't risk it.

I cupped my hand between her legs. "What about here?" My cock was freakishly big like the rest of me. *What if our mating damaged the babe?* Horror streaked through me.

She gave me a teasing smile and rubbed herself against my fingers. "A tiny bit tender, but nothing another orgasm and a quick shift won't fix."

"No!" Doc and I shouted together.

Havana looked between us in confusion. "What?"

Doc let out a deep breath. "Shifting once you are more than a week pregnant can cause a miscarriage. Under no circumstances should you shift for the duration of the pregnancy." Doc reached for her. "Come on out. Let me check you over to make sure everything is okay."

Havana grabbed Doc's hand. "But I've been shifting constantly."

Shit. She'd even taken the hybrid form to save us from the chopper crash yesterday. I helped lift her out of the Jacuzzi, and then followed her and Doc over to one of the lounge chairs.

"All that shifting probably dislodged your IUD and it's why you are pregnant in the first place. Now lie back." Doc helped her recline on the lounger. "How are you feeling right now? Any cramping?"

Cramping? Fuck. I forgot to breathe until Havana shook her head.

I paced restlessly while Doc ran his hands over her lower belly. Besides shifting dozens of times over the past week, she'd battled hordes of zombies yesterday. I hadn't seen her sleep or eat since then. *I should've brought her food. I should've insisted she rest. I shouldn't have mated her like a crazed berserker.*

"Do you have any tenderness or pain?" Doc asked.

Havana shook her head. "Just some nausea, but I've had that since yesterday."

Guilt tore through me. I should have known something was up. I'd chalked up her dizziness and paler complexion to her battles with the dead. I should've known better. Feeling helpless, I watched Doc pull a plastic glove from his pocket and slide it on his hand.

"Do you mind if I do a quick internal exam? I want to make sure there's no bleeding."

Havana arched her eyebrow. "Seriously? You just carry gloves around with you now?"

"I found a whole box of them in the ski lodge clinic. Now lie back and spread your legs."

Havana fluttered her lashes seductively. "I'll spread my legs for you anytime, Dr. James."

"Please, love." Doc knelt and inserted his fingers inside her.

She moaned; although it didn't look like Doc was trying to do anything other than feel her womb.

A few moments later, Doc said, "Your cervix is nice and closed. That's good."

"So good." Havana moaned and thrust her hips against his fingers.

"Stay still," Doc ordered.

"Could move your fingers there... right there?" She rocked her hips restlessly, her eyes going unfocused.

The scent of her growing arousal made my balls tighten.

Doc withdrew his hand and gave her a chiding look. "No, love. You cannot have any orgasms until later in your pregnancy."

I winced. *That's going to suck for all of us.*

Havana sat up. "What? Why the hell not?"

"It causes the muscles of the uterus to contract which can trigger a miscarriage at this early stage."

Havana frowned. "Pregnant women have sex all the time."

Doc pulled off his glove. "Lykos physiology is different from that of human women. Unfortunately, the miscarriage rate is much higher. But don't be upset, love. It's just for the first trimester until the placenta has developed."

Havana pouted. "But that's like twelve weeks."

Doc shook his head. "It's four weeks. A Lykos pregnancy is sixteen weeks to full term. Although it could be a week or so less if it's a multiple pregnancy."

Doc's words gave me pause. *Could she be pregnant with more than one babe?* I liked the idea of twins. I had twin brothers and had always envied the close bond they'd had with one another.

"Multiple pregnancy?" Havana's eyes went wide. "Like instead of one baby, there could be three or four or—?"

Doc interrupted her. "Twin pregnancies occur at a higher rate among Lykos. I'd venture to say one in eight. Higher multiples are much rarer, maybe one in fifty."

Havana let out a deep breath. "Thank God. I was starting to freak out that I'd have a litter of babies."

"That's unlikely. However, there's an ultrasound machine at Sanctuary. As soon as we get back, we'll do a scan." Doc pulled her upright. "I didn't see any blood or negative consequence from your recent interlude with Liam." He gave me a hard look.

Feeling relieved as hell, I grabbed Havana's robe off the floor and handed it to her. "Here, stay warm."

Doc nodded approvingly. "Yes, you'll want to avoid extreme temperatures and you must take in at least twice as many calories as you usually do."

Havana blanched. "I've been pretty nauseous."

"That should fade in the next few days. But until then, you need to eat through the nausea."

"Okay, I'll try." Havana started to stand.

Both Doc and I reached our hands out to help her up.

She laughed and batted us away. "Seriously, guys. I'm fine. You don't need to treat me like some fragile object."

Does she not understand the significance of her condition? All Lykos revered pregnant Alpha females. She was a walking goddess among our kind. Before I could explain that to her, I heard the door opened behind me.

"What the fuck is this?" Nathan's voice boomed.

4

HAVANA

*C*rap. *Not this now.* My nerves were already frayed from trying to process all the information Mason had just dished out. *No shifting. No sex. A decent chance I was carrying twins.* My stomach knotted. It was a lot to wrap my head around. The last thing I needed was Nathan going all Alpha male on us, but it looked as if that was exactly what was happening.

I peered around Liam's massive bicep to find Nathan standing by the door, glaring at the three of us.

The Alpha male's right eye had swollen shut and blood dripped down the side of his bruised jaw.

Oh, God. "Nathan!" I started to run to him, but Mason grabbed my hand, securing me to his side.

"Best give him a minute, love." Mason kissed my hand and gave me a tight smile that didn't quite reach his eyes.

Nathan's red-hot fury exploded through our bond. "Why are you naked? Why is he naked?" He jabbed his finger at Liam.

"I can explain." I quickly threw on the robe. *Do I dare tell Nathan about the pregnancy?*

Liam slowly turned around to look at Nathan, presenting me with a glorious view of his muscular ass. "We're Lykos, we like being naked."

Nathan's amber eyes glinted with rage. "And I'd like to rip your head off and beat you with it, Enforcer."

Mason pulled me closer to him. "This isn't what it looks like, mate."

Nathan's nostrils flared. "Do you think I'm a fucking idiot?" His booming voice reverberated off the water.

"Not at all. You're one of the smartest Lykos I know, Ambassador Steele," Mason said in a soothing voice. He and Liam moved to stand next to one another as if they expected Nathan to attack.

He won't do that. Will he?

Liam apparently thought so. *"Don't make any sudden moves, Beautiful."*

"He'd never hurt me." I knew that with every fiber of my being.

Liam moved so he was physically blocking me from the silver-haired male. *"Not intentionally, but he's out of his mind with jealousy."*

"Alphas are incredibly possessive and seeing you with us may be more than he can handle," added Mason, keeping his gaze on Nathan.

"He's not losing me." I turned to look at Nathan. "You need to calm down. There is nothing for you to be pissed over."

"Pissed doesn't even cover it," Nathan growled. "You're banging two males in here while I'm outside fighting the Enforcer over you." He turned and punched his fist straight into the wall.

I flinched at the sound of his bones breaking. *Oh, Crap.* Technically, I'd only screwed Liam, but I didn't think that would matter to Nathan right now. "Nathan, please." I tried to step around Mason and Liam, but the two males refused to let me pass.

"It's not safe," Liam cautioned, gently pushing me behind him.

He's got to be kidding. "*I can take you all out.*" In my monster-werewolf form, I was huge and virtually indestructible.

"*Remember, you can't shift,*" said Mason.

"*Oh, yeah.*" That sucked.

"We don't want to fight you, Ambassador Steele," Liam said calmly.

"Then you shouldn't have fucked my fiancé, asshole." Nathan bared his teeth, his canines lengthening. His shoulders rippled as the muscles of his back and arm expanded. He looked seconds away from shifting and launching himself at my mates.

Crap.

"The only asshole here is you," Gabriel said, shoving the door open behind Nathan. Moving in a blur of speed, he picked the Alpha male up and threw him into the air.

Nathan flew over our heads and landed in the middle of the pool with a tidal wave-sized splash.

"Some cold water should put out his fire." Gabriel brushed his hands together, a smile of satisfaction on his face.

"Nice one, brother," Liam said, offering the dark-haired male a high-five.

Nathan stayed under the water long enough that my heart took on a frantic beat inside my chest.

Just as I was getting ready to dive in after him, he surfaced and swam for the edge of the pool.

Relieved Nathan was okay and the tense situation seemed diffused for the moment, I sidestepped around Mason to get a better look at Gabriel. The smooth bronze skin of his broad, muscular chest was unmarked, and the chiseled features of his face were perfect. Unlike Nathan, it seemed the dark-haired male had come out of the fight without a scratch.

Gabriel sniffed in my direction, then smiled. "Why didn't you invite me to the fuck fest, Princess?"

I put my hands on my hips. "You were too busy beating Nathan's face in." My frosty tone could have turned the pool into a skating rink.

Gabriel's cocky expression faded. "You're angry?"

"Fuck yeah, I'm angry," shouted Nathan. It sounded as if he were pulling himself out of the water.

"Stay over there, Nathan," I yelled, putting a healthy amount of compulsion in the order. I didn't want him coming back and starting more shit with my mates.

Turning my attention back to Gabriel, I said, "I asked you and Nathan not to fight." Switching to our telepathic channel, I added, *"It ruined the celebration."* That wasn't entirely true, but he deserved to feel some guilt.

Gabriel blinked. "Did I really?" His gaze went to Liam.

My giant mate nodded. "You upset her. You need to apologize."

"For fuck's sake. He needs to apologize to me," boomed Nathan.

We all ignored the Alpha.

"She made it clear she didn't want fighting between you and Ambassador Steele," Mason said in a low voice. "Instead of supporting her, you went against her wishes."

Gabriel crossed his arms over his chest. "But that motherfucker openly challenged me."

"No one can take on an Alpha and win," Nathan called out.

I rolled my eyes willing Nathan to shut the hell up.

"It doesn't matter, Gabe. If Havana said no fighting Nathan, we don't fight Nathan."

I gave Liam a look of thanks.

Gabriel still wore a defiant expression. "But Nathan—"

Liam interrupted him. "Do you want Havana to unclaim you and throw you out of her faction?"

"Yes!" Nathan shouted.

I gave Liam a quick look. *That's a little harsh.*

My biggest mate kept his gaze on Gabriel. *It's the only way to get through his stubborn skull.*

Gabriel looked startled for a moment. "No, that's the last thing I want." He fell to his knees in front of me. "I swear not to disobey you again." His regret pulsed through our bond as he kissed my feet.

"It's okay, baby." I held my hand out to him.

Instead of pulling himself up with it, Gabriel kissed my hand all the while keeping his eyes downcast.

"It's okay," I reached out and caressed the dark stubble on his chin.

"None of this is fucking okay," shouted Nathan.

I gave the annoying Alpha the finger with my free hand. To Gabriel, I said, "I know it's hard when someone is trying to start shit." *Hell.* At that moment, I kind of wanted to punch Nathan in the face too.

Gabriel finally looked up, his beautiful dark eyes meeting mine. "So you're not mad at me?"

"No." There was no way I could stay angry with him. Gabriel was a moody, cynical bastard, but he was as loyal as they came. I knew he'd never knowingly do anything to cause me pain. Unless I asked for it... Memories of his spankings and nipple pinching came to mind. I ran my hand across his full lips.

Gabriel nipped my fingers lightly.

Just like that a haze of desire wiped any other thought from my mind. That clawing, aching need I thought I'd satisfied with Liam came roaring back. I let out that strange half growl-half purr sound again. "You'll definitely need to be punished though."

Gabriel's lips curled. "What punishment did you have in mind?"

Heat flared between my legs. "Make me forget my name." Uncaring of our audience, I slid my thigh over his shoulder and pressed myself against his face.

"Unfucking believable!" Nathan shouted from across the room. It sounded as if he was punching the wall again.

I didn't give a crap about him because Gabriel was gripping my ass in his hands and giving my pussy a toe-curling lick that had me shrieking in delight.

"Yes!" I buried my fingers in his thick dark hair. I needed this so bad. I moaned, feeling Mason and Liam's hands on my body. *Yes!* I wanted them all touching me while Gabriel pleasured me, then I wanted each of them to take me one right after another—

Mason physically ripped me off Gabriel. "You can't."

"No!" I cried out as the Omega set me down on a lounge chair. "I need—" A feverish hunger had me trying to pull Mason on top of me.

He backed away. "No, love. Remember, you can't do this."

Mason's words were like a slap on the face. *He's right. Crap. "Mason, what the fuck is wrong with me?"* My breath came in pants as I tried to get ahold of myself.

Mason's brows drew together. *"Surges in hormones can lead to an increased sex drive in some pregnant females."*

This went far beyond an increased sex drive. The need to come was almost physically painful. I fought the urge to slip my hand between my legs. *Get a grip, Vana.*

"Why can't she mate?" Gabriel asked, shoving Liam. Apparently, the big guy had pulled Gabriel away.

I can't believe I just jumped on his face. A wave of embarrassment washed over me. Too bad it did nothing to dull the throbbing ache between my legs.

Gabriel wore a confused expression. "It looks as though she's in heat again."

"She's not," Liam and Mason said at the same time.

"She's pregnant," Nathan announced in a pained voice.

We all turned our head to find the Alpha male staring at me, a stricken look on his face. "Tasha would sometimes get like this—"

"Soon after she conceived," Gabriel finished for him. He stood, his dark eyes filling with wonder. "You're pregnant." He walked over to where I sat and crouched down next to me. "This is a blessing." He laid one hand over my abdomen.

I smiled and covered his hand with my own. "It is." Even though the timing couldn't be more off, at least Liam, Mason, and Gabriel seemed excited about it.

"Who's the father?" Nathan demanded.

I tensed. *Good question. How will we know?*

"*We don't need to know,*" Liam said, reading my mind. "It's ours."

Mason nodded his head. "Ours."

"Ours," Gabriel repeated, rubbing my belly.

His fingers on my skin fueled the fire in my blood. Trying to control the sexual hunger before it took over again, I pushed Gabriel's hand away and stood. "We'll raise this child, and all the others, together... as a family."

Nathan cursed. "Then I see you've made your choice." He'd lost his blanket in the pool and tiny rivulets of water dripped down his gorgeous, naked muscular body.

Damn, he's as sexy as ever. I wet my lips. "My choice is to have all four of you as my mates."

Nathan shook his head. "I can't go for that."

Anger sparked inside me. "Well, you don't get to make all the decisions anymore."

Nathan looked stunned. "You compelled me to accept your claim and now you'd force me to stay with you?"

My mates stared at me in shocked silence.

"You compelled him to bond with you?" Gabriel finally asked.

"Well, yeah, I had to."

I felt Liam and Gabriel's immediate shock and horror. It was clear I'd violated some sacred rule. I tried to explain. "I had to in order to save his life."

Nathan slapped his chest. "You accomplished your goal. I'm alive and I don't want to spend the rest of my days as one of your groupies. Unclaim me."

I sucked in a pained breath. *He can't mean that.* Some part of me hoped against hope he'd be willing to give this a try. "Nathan, I want you and them. We can all be together."

"No, we can't," he spat. "I'm not sharing with these males."

I let out an exasperated breath. "Why are you being so stubborn? When we first got together you wanted to share me with Tyberius, remember?" A memory of Nathan's model-gorgeous best friend flashed in my mind. My temple throbbed for a second and another memory, or maybe it was a dream, flashed in my head. The tall, dark-skinned male was reading to me from a book. Tyberius looked over the top of the pages. *"I love you, Starfire."*

I blinked and the memory or dream faded.

Weird.

Nathan clenched his jaw. "That was different."

"Different how?" I put my hands on my hips. "At the time I'd never had a threesome, but I was willing to give it a try for you. Why can't you try this for me?"

My other mates look from me to Nathan.

"No." Nathan's expression hardened. "Release me from your claim."

I shook my head. I didn't want to lose him, not now after I'd just gotten him back. "Nathan, please."

"If you don't let me go, you're no better than Tasha."

I recoiled from his words and the hurt and anger radiating from our bond.

"She's nothing like Tasha," Liam declared stepping in front of me.

I gave him a grateful look.

Gabriel growled. "The fact you'd ever even make that comparison tells me you don't deserve our Alpha. If you want your freedom, she'll give it to you. Right, Havana?"

I slowly nodded, anguish tearing at my heart. "Are you sure, Nathan?" He'd told me once I broke the bond, it could never be remade.

His golden gaze arrowed straight into my soul. "Are *you* sure, Vana? You're throwing away everything we had, our love, our family, our future for them." He jabbed his finger at my other mates. "You don't even know them."

I looked into Gabriel's dark eyes, then Liam's deep green ones, and then finally Mason's ocean blue gaze. "I know enough. I know I love each of them, just as I love you."

A pained look crossed Nathan's face. "Choose me and only me, or let me go."

Grief choked me, but I couldn't force Nathan to stay with me and I wouldn't leave the males who'd fathered my child. I swallowed hard. "W-what do I do to break the bond?"

Nathan's face lost color. He obviously hadn't expected me to choose the others over him.

Liam, Gabriel, and Mason looked at each other with uncertain expressions.

"I think you just declare him to be unclaimed," Liam finally said.

Fine. "I unclaim you, Nathan Steele." I held my breath,

waiting for something to happen. Nothing did. "That didn't work."

"Try reversing the claiming by telling him he isn't yours," Mason said.

"You're not mine," I called out.

Nathan flinched, but our bond felt no different. If anything, I could feel his anguish and pain more intensely.

"What am I doing wrong?"

Gabriel shrugged and Liam shook his head. They were no help.

Mason gave me a sad look. "I'm sorry, love. Unclaimings are very rare. I've never seen one."

I looked over at Nathan. "Well? Why isn't it working?"

"You have to mean it," he replied softly.

Well, hell. Tears sprang into my eyes. I tried to blink them away. "I-I need a minute." I took a deep breath and walked to the door.

Liam, Mason, and Gabriel tried to follow.

"I want to be alone." When the guys didn't stop, I held up my hand. "Please. I'll just be out in the hallway."

"Can you release your compulsion? I'd like to walk to the other side of the room?" Nathan asked, refusing to meet my gaze.

"As long as there's no fighting." I glanced between him and Gabriel.

Gabriel looked in Nathan's direction. "That won't be a problem, right Ambassador?"

Nathan let out a cold laugh. "I've got no reason to fight now."

"Then be free." With my bitter words ringing in my ears, I slipped out into the hallway.

❦ 5 ❦

NATHAN

The love of my life walked out of the room and slammed the door on my hopes and dreams.

Damn the fucking fates to hell. Pain exploded inside my chest as if my heart had been ripped out through my sternum. The Beast had actually done that to me many years ago. The suffering had been so intense I'd begged Tasha for death. Never had I experienced as much pain. *Until now.*

Vana tried to unclaim me.

I let out a ragged breath. Never did I imagine she'd choose three strangers over me. I'd been wrong. *So very wrong.*

My hand shook as I rubbed it across my throbbing face. Blood wet my fingers and left a salty, bitter taste in my mouth.

I knew I needed to shift and heal the damage, but I couldn't summon the energy.

I've lost my chosen. My mate. My Vana. Never again would I watch her giggle with Mira, share stories with her over dinner, or wake tangled in her long dark hair.

All my plans to build a life with her were nothing but

dust. My inner wolf wanted to howl in sorrow. For months, the only thing that kept me going was the hope that we'd be reunited. And now she belonged to the males I'd mistakenly trusted with her care.

Those fuckers.

I gnashed my teeth and glared at Gabriel, Liam, and Mason.

They watched me with wary expressions.

They betrayed me. They took my mate. They planted their seed inside her.

Grief and anger unlike anything I'd ever experienced gripped me. In an explosion of rage, I charged across the pool deck at my rivals.

The doctor was the closest.

I leapt for him.

Gabriel pushed Mason out of my path and faced me. "Get ahold of yourself."

"This is for taking my chosen." I drove my fist into his jaw.

Gabriel's head snapped back and blood flew from his mouth.

"I trusted her with you." I slammed my fist into his stomach.

He doubled over, but didn't even try to avoid my next punch.

"Fight me!" I shouted.

Gabriel shook his head, blood dripping from his split lip.

"He won't go against Havana's wishes," Liam called out.

Fuck! I spun around to face the redheaded giant. "You fight me!"

"No," Liam replied.

"Fight me!" I reared back to punch him in the face.

Liam didn't move a muscle. He looked over my shoulder at Gabriel. "Didn't we always call him the calm one?"

Fuck calm. My fist connected with his face. Pain exploded from my bleeding knuckles. *Damnation.* "Is your head made from stone, you oversized piece of shit."

Liam had the gall to smile at me.

"In Nathan's defense, he nearly died yesterday," Mason said to the other two males.

It might have been better if I had died. Letting out a howl of frustration, I picked up the closest lounge chair and hurled it at Liam. "Fight me!"

The chair bounced off the giant who stood there, a look of pity on his face.

From my deepest subconscious, I heard my long dead father's voice. *"Let them envy you, let them fear you, but never let them pity you."*

I straightened my spine. "You're cowards, all three of you!"

Mason shook his head. "Havana doesn't want us fighting."

"We do what she says," Liam added.

"She is our mate, our Alpha, the mother of our young," finished Gabriel.

Chest heaving, I looked between the three of them. They were all tall, good-looking, and strong. *No wonder Vana chose them over you.* I shut my eyes against the pent up rage, frustration, and grief.

For decades I'd only ever known pain. The plunge of Tasha's knife into my flesh. The bite of her barbed cat-o'-nine-tails. The gnawing ache of my belly as I starved near to death, shackled to the wall of her dining room. I'd endured it all, but this... losing my chosen to Tasha's henchmen was too much.

My knees gave out and I collapsed. Exhaustion replaced the anger slowly seeping out of me. I hung my head. "Vana is everything to me."

"You have a shit way of showing it." Gabriel slid off his

pants and transformed in and out of his wolf faster than I could blink. He touched his newly healed lip and scowled at me. "That hurt."

"Good," I spat. I knew I was acting like an asshole, but I'd trusted him to bring my fiancé to safety, not mate her and impregnate her. He deserved to feel some of the pain I was feeling.

Liam bent down and picked something off of the floor. "Havana is still in love with you Nathan." He held up the engagement ring I'd given Vana and offered it to me.

The wound in my chest ripped open again. I refused to take it from him. "Throw it away. It means nothing now." The half a million-dollar stone that I'd flown across the country to purchase for her could rot at the bottom of the pool for all I cared.

Liam curled his hand around the ring. "An hour ago she told me she wants to marry you."

What? I blinked at him.

Mason and Gabriel gave him a WTF look.

Liam cleared his throat. "She wants to marry us in a human ceremony. All four of us."

Mason chuckled. "We'll have to look for a priest among the survivors."

"She wouldn't want a religious ceremony," I replied before I could stop myself. Vana had confessed she'd lost all faith in religion when her mother died. I'd been planning an outdoor night wedding for us. I knew how much she loved stargazing from her dates with Ty.

I took a deep breath and pushed myself to my feet. I guess that was one of a million things I no longer needed to remember. Along with the fact she liked her coffee black, her French fries cold, and subtitles on for all the movies we watched.

"Right," Mason said slowly. "You know Havana far better than we do."

I snorted. "We spent nearly every waking minute together for months, you spent what? A week with her? Good luck keeping her happy."

Gabriel narrowed his gaze. "I'm more worried about keeping Havana alive. She's a pregnant Alpha female in the Beast's territory. What do you think Tasha will do to her?"

The memory of Tasha poised with a knife over my newborn daughter pierced my heart. "I won't let the Beast hurt Vana." Even though Vana's choice wounded me deeper than I wanted to admit, I'd never let harm come to her. Nor could I ever leave her. *She's my chosen.*

"How will you keep her safe?"

I debated sharing my plans with these males. I didn't owe them shit, but their loyalty to Vana could prove useful. *Damn the fates.* I took a deep breath and summoned my calm political alter ego. "The southwest faction Alphas and the high council are convening at Sanctuary at the end of the week."

Gabriel's brow furrowed. "Are you talking about Tasha's New Year's Eve Party?"

I nodded. For the better part of a year, Ty and I had been plotting to bring down Tasha at the celebration.

"I can't imagine there will be any party considering current world events," Mason interjected.

He's wrong. "Because of the outbreak, it will be even more imperative that council meet. Since the gathering at Sanctuary was already underway, it's unlikely the meeting would be held elsewhere. Of course, I've been out of the loop for ten days." I looked down at my aching fist. The skin around my swollen knuckles was shredded and the small movement made blood drip down my arm.

"I don't understand." Gabriel took a step forward. "How

would the other Alphas and council members keep Havana safe?"

I shook the blood off. "I've convinced the Moon Valley faction, the Red Canyon faction, and several council members to join forces with me." I let that sink in and then said, "Together we'll take out Tasha."

The Head Enforcer let out a laugh that reverberated off the high ceiling. "You think you could just kill the Beast? Did you learn nothing from all those years as her prisoner?"

"Tasha can't be killed," Liam added as if I didn't know that.

"Not kill her," I corrected. Like the two Enforcers, I'd seen Tasha anticipate and evade every attempt on her life, but her foresight seemed limited to immediate physical threats. "This is a political maneuver." Even Tasha couldn't defy pressure from the council and her neighboring factions to step down. "Once Tasha is forced to abdicate, she'll lose her power."

"She's an Original," Liam blurted out.

Fair point. "But an Original with no faction is much easier dealt with." Once Tasha could no longer order the Winterhaven Enforcers to fight for her, she'd be vulnerable. Or at least as vulnerable as an immortal monster could be. "Ty's been designing something to incarcerate her."

Gabriel and Liam exchanged a quick look.

"What?" *Am I missing something?*

Gabriel cleared his throat. "Two weeks ago, Tasha ordered Tyberius back to Winterhaven and imprisoned him."

Ah, fucking hell. I'd wondered why I couldn't reach him. Tasha probably had him in her silver reinforced dungeon. *Damnation.* I knew Tasha would never kill her son, but she'd make his life a living hell.

"She'll torture him until she discovers your plan," Liam added.

Before worry for my friend could distract me, I shook my head. "Ty will never tell her what we have planned. I would stake my life on that." Once we'd removed Tasha as the faction leader, I'd free Ty and he'd never have to go into that hellhole again.

"After Tasha steps down—"

Gabriel's snorted.

I cleared my throat and continued, "After Tasha steps down, the Moon Valley Alpha will nominate Mira as the Winterhaven Alpha. Ty and I will act as regents until she's of age." I dragged in a breath. The next part of my plan, where Vana and I established a home together in Winterhaven, was nothing but a pipe dream now.

"What about Havana?" Liam asked, looking down at the engagement ring in his hand.

"That's up to her." A phantom knife wrenched inside my gut.

"She'll establish her own faction at Sanctuary," Gabriel announced.

I started to argue, but then closed my mouth. If she were at Sanctuary I'd still get to see her. My chest tightened. "Fine."

"You're putting the cart before the horse here," Mason said. "What are the chances Nathan's plan will even work?"

"The plan will work." *It had to.*

"And if it doesn't?" Gabriel said in a low voice.

I closed my eyes at that horrifying outcome. "Then, the Moon Valley Alpha has offered Vana and Mira refuge in her territory." There was no point in Shoshanna offering me refuge as I'd be rotting in Tasha's dungeon by that point.

Gabriel scrubbed a hand across his chin. "And where were you planning on stashing Mira and Havana while your grand plans were going down?"

"Ty was supposed to take them far from here." Clearly,

that wasn't going to happen now. "One of you can take them instead."

Gabriel shook his head. "We can't risk Havana traveling in her condition."

"Pregnant, she's too vulnerable," added Mason.

I flinched at the reminder of Vana's condition. "Then we'll have her and Mira stay here with the humans."

"Mason will stay and protect them." Gabriel nodded over at Liam. "Liam and I will help you. We'll return to Tasha, rejoin the Enforcers and help take her down from within." Gabriel rubbed his right eye as if it pained him.

Their offer was attractive, unfortunately it would be impossible for them to get near Tasha. "The Beast will smell that you've mated a mile away." Even now, I could scent Vana all over them.

"You carry Havana's scent too," Liam pointed out.

I looked at the door. "Not once she unclaims me." Not that I wanted her to. *Damnation, why can't she choose me?*

The three males exchanged long looks. It was clear they were conversing telepathically.

Gabriel finally cleared his throat. "As much as I hate to admit it, Mason, you're right."

It was my turn to give them a wary look. "What are you talking about?"

Mason turned and looked at me. "Havana will need your leadership experience and counsel to rule her faction."

Gabriel and Liam nodded.

I shook my head "I want no part of this." I waved my hand between them. The very idea of sharing Vana with others left a bitter taste in my mouth.

But wasn't it fucking hot when Gabriel went down on Vana? I shook my head in denial at that unbidden thought.

Gabriel cocked his head to the side. "You enjoyed watching me with Havana."

Fuck! I must be very weak if the Enforcer could read my thoughts so easily. "No!" I shouted a little too loud.

The Enforcer grinned. "Stay with us and we'll give you a live action show any time you want."

"No," I said again. *Fuck.* The mental image of the males taking Vana in front of me made my cock twitch.

Liam slowly nodded. "There were rumors about him and Tyberius. Apparently, Nathan liked to watch while Ty—"

I jumped to my feet. My voyeuristic tendencies were my business. "I'm done with this conversation." *To hell with waiting for Vana.* I started for the door.

"What about Miss Mira?" Mason called out.

I whirled around. "What about my daughter?"

"She adores Havana. She was just telling me how you three were all going to live together and have slumber parties every night."

Damnation. Mira had been inconsolable when Vana disappeared from her life the first time. *Can I separate them again?*

"You should stay for your daughter's sake," Gabriel said, twisting the knife.

Damn the fates.

"You still love Havana, right?" Liam asked.

I jerked my head in his direction. "That's a stupid question. I'd give my life for her." If she walked back into the room and said she'd changed her mind and chose me over these males, I'd drag her into my arms and never let her go.

Gabriel crossed over to where I stood. "But you won't share her."

I growled at him. "No."

"Why not?" asked Liam, walking around me in a half circle.

I hesitated not knowing how to explain that I'd had nothing that truly belonged to me. *Until Vana.*

"But wouldn't you enjoy watching us share her?" Gabriel

sent telepathic images of him and Liam tying Vana down, spanking her, and mounting her in front of me. In his vision, I was instructing them on what to do to her.

I inhaled sharply, a bolt of lust kicking me in the balls. The very idea of it tempted me beyond reason. *Am I actually considering this?*

"Havana has a voracious sexual appetite, mate," Mason added.

Liam nodded. "The three of us aren't enough for her. She needs you."

"She needs you," the other two males said in unison. "Serve her."

Their words hit some primal internal bull's-eye. To be needed by a female was the fundamental drive of a male Lykos and to serve an Alpha female was the highest calling. Pride be damned. Alpha possessiveness be damned. *Vana needs me. And I need her too.* "I'd be in charge?"

Gabriel didn't answer right away.

"Yes, you'd be the Head Mate," Liam gave Gabriel a hard look and mouthed, "He's the Alpha, brother."

"Fine, yes," Gabriel gritted out.

Mason smiled. "Then it's agreed. You'll stay."

Not so fast. "We've only begun the negotiating process." I gestured at the closest table. Working through deals was what I did best.

The males looked from the table back to me.

"Sit," I ordered. "And we'll discuss the terms of this arrangement."

❧ 6 ❧

HAVANA

Pacing the worn carpeted hallway outside the door to the pool wasn't doing anything to soothe my nerves. Even worse, that horrible feeling of impending doom slammed back into me the moment I'd left my mates.

As I stalked by the ice machine, I turned inward searching for some hint of where the danger lay. My mates and I were safe, for the moment at least. *Where's the threat?*

Not in the lobby where the sounds of giggling children and arguing humans could be heard. Not in this hallway that carried the odor of decay and musty wet carpet. I opened all my senses straining to pick up some hint of danger.

There was nothing.

Deciding I had enough problems without some irrational fear weighing down on me, I mentally shoved all my anxiety into an invisible box and closed the lid.

Now to solve my romantic situation. I didn't want to lose Nathan, but I also couldn't abandon my other mates.

Why is Nathan being such a stubborn ass?

I balled my hands up in frustration. Nathan loved me. They loved me. I was pretty confident I could keep all four of them sexually satisfied. I pressed my thighs together, trying to ease the insistent ache of my lady blue balls.

So why can't we all live together happily-ever-after?

When Nathan had initially demanded I choose between them, he'd asked me how I'd like it if the situation was reversed. Although the notion of sharing Nathan with three other women made me want to chew glass, I might have been willing to try it if it meant we could still be together. *Why won't he at least try?*

Instead, he wanted me to unclaim him and destroy any possible future between us. *What am I going to do?*

I couldn't force Nathan to stay with me. *Or can I?*

A dark voice, one I hardly recognized, whispered inside my head, *"I can compel him to stay."*

No. I shook my head immediately rejecting the horrific idea. I'd never force someone to be with me. Even if this break up shattered my heart.

The sound of Mira's laughter filtered in from the lobby. I stopped and closed my eyes. The idea of never seeing that sassy little girl again physically pained me. I loved her, just as I loved her father. If Tasha hadn't stormed Nathan's house months ago, he and I would probably be married and I'd be Mira's stepmother.

I reached into my robe pocket. Nathan's engagement ring wasn't there.

Crap. I turned the pocket inside out before realizing I'd never picked it up when it'd dropped near the pool. By now the ring could've fallen into a drain or something.

God damn it. I turned and kicked the bottom of the ice machine.

The loud thud echoed in the hallway along with my curse of pain.

I inspected my bruised toes. *Ouch.* Without the ability to shift and heal myself, I'd have to rein in my temper.

"Vana!"

I turned to see Mira standing at the end of the hallway. I forced a smile. "Hi, bug."

"I don't feel so good," she said rubbing the back of her neck.

Concern for her wiped away my frustration. "What's wrong?"

"My neck feels funny."

I let out the breath I was holding. "Remember Mason said you might have whiplash. That would make your neck and back sore." The helicopter had crashed hard. It was amazing she'd walked away with only a few cuts and bruises. I walked over to her. "Does it hurt when you move your neck?"

"No." She rotated her head from side to side so fast the butterfly hairpin went flying. "Oh, no!" She bent over to pick it up.

Even though she couldn't be that seriously injured, I decided to insist Mason do another examination. "We'll have Mason take a look at your neck, okay?"

"He gave me this hairloom." She held up the hairpin. "Look. It's a butterfly."

"It's beautiful," I said, trying not to laugh at her mispronunciation. "Let me put it back in."

"Okay." Mira handed me the hairpiece.

The walnut-sized diamond butterfly was stunning, but I hadn't realized that the gold pin was a good three inches long. "You must be careful with this, bug." I didn't want her hurting herself with it.

"I will," she promised. She stood still while I swept her long tangled mane into a knot and slid in the pin. With her red turtleneck and topknot, she looked far older than her years.

"There, you look just like a princess."

"Yay," she squealed. "I want to show Daddy. Where is he?"

I glanced over at the door to the pool. "He's at the pool right now—"

"Pool!" she shrieked. "Can I go swimming? I want to go swimming!"

"What about your neck?"

"It's fine. I want to go! Can I go? Please! Please!"

"All right then." I laughed. "Assuming Mason approves, you can go swimming.

"Yes!" she jumped up and down. "Can we go now?"

"Um." I glanced back at the pool door remembering Nathan and Liam's lack of clothing. "Let's check the luggage behind the front desk for some swim clothes." *And some clothes for the guys.*

"I want one that's pink and has a unicorn on it."

"Let's see what we can do," I said, letting her drag me to the lobby. "Why don't you tell the boys about the pool while I go look through the luggage?"

"Okay!" She darted off to the Christmas tree where the boys sat sucking on candy canes bigger than their faces.

Ugh. They were all going to be sticky messes. A dip in the pool was definitely in order.

I looked over at the rest of the survivors. Most stood near the front desk still arguing in low voices. *Seriously?* I rolled my eyes. Maybe a dip in the pool might improve their moods too.

Shaking my head, I stepped behind the front desk. An explosion of clothing and toiletry items covered the floor. I sighed wishing I'd been a little neater when I'd search the bags for Christmas gifts.

Despite the mess, I located a pair of jogging pants I thought might fit Nathan. Liam was out of luck, but I found a girl's swimsuit somewhat close to Mira's size. I walked around the front desk and brought the turquoise suit over to where Mira stood talking to the boys.

"Look what I found, bug. It has mermaids on it."

"I love it!" Mira snatched it out of my hands. "I want to go swimming now!"

Kaden and Jackson threw down their candy canes. "We want to go too!"

"Shh! Inside voices," hissed Rebecca, patting the now sleeping Sierra's back. The woman sat on the closest windowsill, her watchful gaze on the children.

The little ones immediately quieted.

Rebecca nodded her approval. "If you're good and sit down criss-cross applesauce, maybe all of us can go swimming in a little bit."

All three kids immediately sat down.

Man. I can learn a thing or two from that lady. "I'm going to let the guys know the plan." *And make sure they get some clothes on.* As I turned to leave, Marshall intercepted me.

"Hey, legs. Do you know where Nathan went?"

I bristled, not liking the older man's demeaning nickname or his demanding tone. "Yes."

When I didn't elaborate, he scowled, and rubbed the hawkish point of his nose. "Tell him we're not leaving here."

My hands involuntarily curled into fists. "Is that so?"

Rebecca stood and marched over to the balding man. "Our best chance of survival is to stick with Nathan and his friends."

Go Rebecca.

"No," Marshall replied. "Our best chance of survival is to wait for help."

The man was delusional if he thought help was on its way. If what my mates had told me was true, all of human civilization had fallen. No one was coming to save us. We'd have to save ourselves.

Rebecca clearly felt the same. "There's no help coming, Marshall. I trust Nathan's judgment. He's the only reason any of us are alive. If he says we go, we go."

"No." Marshall's face turned beet red and the vein on the side of his liver-spotted temple throbbed. "Help will come."

Enough. I caught his eye. "Marshall, you will—"

Rebecca interrupted my attempt at compulsion. "If you stay you'll either starve or you'll become lunch for the next horde of zombies. Now stop leering at Havana, take that self-righteous stick out of your ass, and tell the others to get their things together."

Marshall gaped at Rebecca like a dying fish. Likely, no one had ever talked down to him like that in his entire rich and powerful life.

I freaking loved this woman. Deciding Rebecca had it well enough in hand, I tucked the jogging pants under my arm and headed back to the pool.

Poor Marshall. He was still clinging to the rules of the old world. The world where police officers and soldiers protected us from the bad guys. Although it would be hard, Marshall would eventually adapt to our new reality.

Just like Nathan would eventually adapt to my mates. Discovering I was mated to his friends and pregnant to boot was a lot to handle. *Nathan just needs some time to adjust.*

I'd give him that time, and I'd try to be patient with him. But I would not break our bond. Not now. Not ever.

Squaring my shoulders, I pushed the door to the pool open. I'm not sure what I expected to find, but it wasn't all four of my mates seated at a small patio table deep in discussion. It was strange, but definitely better than finding them at each other's throats. "What's going on, guys?"

The four guilty expressions didn't give me the warm fuzzies. I walked over and set the jogging pants in front of Nathan. "What are you all talking about?"

No one said anything for a heartbeat, and then Nathan said, "We're discussing the terms of me staying."

I blinked in surprise. "Terms? What terms?"

"We've agreed to put Nathan in charge," Mason called out.

"He's Head Mate," added Liam, who'd already put back on his jeans.

Head mate? "What does that mean?"

"It means they are under my command." Nathan stood, his rugged face perfectly healed. Damn he was sexy with that silvery beard. Even without one of his four thousand dollar suits on, he exuded so much power and confidence, I was irresistibly drawn to him.

I looked up at him through my eyelashes. "Am I under your command too?"

His eyes blazed a mesmerizing shade of amber. "If only."

"So you'll stay?" I searched his face and our bond for some hint at his emotions.

He was completely closed down. "For the time being." He pulled on the jogging pants.

"I'm so glad. We'll make this work. You won't regret this." I tried to kiss him, but he turned toward the others.

"And our agreement stands?" he said to my three other mates.

They all nodded like obedient lap dogs.

I looked at them in confusion. "What agreement?"

Mason stood. "Besides him being Head Mate, he gets to sleep with you alone a minimum of three days a week. He gets to have lunch with you and Mira alone five days a week."

"And he gets first mating when you are in heat," added Liam.

"And Nathan gets to watch us mate whenever he wants," Gabriel said through gritted teeth.

What? "And you decided all of this without me?" *What about my thoughts and feelings?*

All four of my mates nodded with a male arrogance that infuriated me.

As anger simmered inside me, I curled my hands into fists. "What if I don't agree to these terms?"

Nathan opened his mouth to say something, but the sound of a woman's scream interrupted him.

We all jerked around.

Another scream rang out from outside the door.

"Oh, no! What's happening?" *Are the survivors under attack?* I ran for the door.

"You stay here." Gabriel grabbed my arm. "Liam and I will check it out."

Nathan stepped in front of him. "I'm in charge, remember? Vana, you stay here with Mason. Liam and Gabriel, you're with me."

"Wait. I can fight too," Mason shouted.

The other males shoved past him and left Mason and I alone in the room.

"It's probably nothing, love," Mason said, pushing me behind him. He scanned the room and ran over to the long metal pool net mounted on the wall. After pulling it down, he forcefully snapped off the net and held up the pole as if it were a spear.

I opened my robe, preparing to shift into my monster werewolf form before remembering I couldn't. *Crap.*

Nathan's horror, panic, and grief blasted me, nearly bringing me to my knees. *"Nathan! What is it?"*

He didn't respond, but there was only one thing that would make him lose it like that.

Mira! "Something's happened to Mira."

The door swung open.

Liam stood in the doorway, his face pale. "Doc, we need you."

"What's happened?" I shrieked. "Is Mira okay?"

His bleak expression froze my blood. "She's infected."

❦   7   ❦

MASON

My heart raced as Havana and I rushed after Liam down the hallway. *How could the little Alpha be infected?* Mira seemed in fine health just an hour ago when she'd adamantly refused to give up the champagne.

"Did zombies break in?" Hysteria made Havana's voice tight.

"Nothing like that," Liam called back. His long strides ate up the hallway, making both Havana and I jog to keep up. In seconds we reached the lobby.

The humans were huddled near the fireplace, their horror-filled gazes on the small swimsuit clad Alpha female.

Mira squirmed in her father's arms. "Let me down, Daddy. I didn't do anything wrong."

"I know, sunshine," Nathan said in a choked voice.

"Keep her away from us," shouted Marshall. "She could infect us all."

"Be quiet!" Although Gabriel's tone was no nonsense, his gaze never left Mira's back. As we grew closer, I saw why.

Long tendrils of black veins streaked down the little girl's spine.

Bloody hell. The vascular necrosis was unmistakable. Somehow the little girl had contracted the Z-virus.

Havana let out a gasp and sprinted over to Nathan and Mira. "Oh no, baby!" Tears ran down her face as she threw her arms around Mira and Nathan. "How did this happen?"

"I don't know," Nathan said, his voice tighter than a bow. "She was fine yesterday at the lodge. It must've happened after Liam took her." He glared at the redheaded Enforcer.

Liam stopped a few feet away. A look of guilt and pain crossed his face. "I didn't... I don't ..."

Mira pushed away from her father and jumped into Havana's arms. "You said I could swim. I want to swim."

"And you will, bug," Havana said with forced cheer. "But first we need to look at your back. Does it hurt?" She rubbed her fingers over the dark veins.

Mira shook her head.

I stopped next to them. "Do you mind if I look, Miss Mira?"

The child blinked at me with her large golden eyes. "Okay, but I'm not giving you my juice."

"Of course," I said, trying to keep my tone light. I swept my gaze over her body trying to locate the origin of the infection.

Havana shifted Mira so I could see more of her upper back. "Mira's been complaining that her neck felt funny. But I never thought..."

It took only a second to find the origin of the infection— a small laceration no bigger than a thumbnail near the base of her skull. The necrosis radiated from the superficial injury that, under any other circumstances, would have healed without a scar. *Christ*. I'd missed the small injury during my exam of Mira yesterday, but even if I'd seen it, the Z-virus was initially impossible to identify with the naked eye.

Havana let out a sob. "A horde of zombies attacked the

helicopter before I could take them out. They smashed the windows... One must've scratched Mira. Oh, God." She started hyperventilating.

I put my arm around her. "Deep breaths, love." We didn't need Havana collapsing.

Mira pursed her lips. "What's wrong with my back? Am I sick?"

Havana drew in a steadying breath and schooled her face into a smile. "Yes, bug, but Mason will cure you just like he cured me."

Nathan, who'd been standing frozen, broke from his stupor. "You can fix this, Wheeler?"

This wasn't the time to remind him of my new surname. I opened my mouth and then closed it when I realized he'd go mental when he discovered the truth.

Havana grabbed my arm. "Mason, you can help her, right?" Her fingers dug into my arm painfully.

If only that were the case. True, I'd been able to accelerate Havana's first Lykos transition with Tasha's blood. However, Havana had been just days away from her first transition. Mira was over a decade away from hers. Until she could take wolf form, she would be just as vulnerable to the virulent Z-virus as human children. The best I could do was ease the little girl's imminent passing.

The smell of fear wafting off the humans grew stronger. It was in their and Mira's best interest, that we moved her away from them.

I took a deep breath and summoned my years of experience interacting with bereaved family members. "I'll do my very best. Now let's get Mira somewhere more private."

Gabriel glanced out the window. "What about the clinic next door?"

"Perfect. We can treat her there." I looked over at the front desk. "I'll need my messenger bag."

"We'll get you everything you need," Nathan said, his eyes filled with desperate hope. He turned to Gabriel. "Go get my daughter's clothes. She says she left them in the women's restroom."

Gabriel inclined his head and headed toward the bathroom.

Nathan looked over at Liam. "Get Mason's bag."

Liam nodded and strode over to the front desk.

Havana set Mira down. "We're going to the lodge, bug."

"No!" The little Alpha stamped her foot. "I want to go swimming!" Tears sprang into her eyes. "You promised!"

"You're right I did," Havana said, facing down the mini tornado. "And we will go swimming right after you get a checkup. We can even get more crayons from the gift shop on our way."

"I want crayons. Can I go with Mira?" shouted Kaden, jumping to his feet.

"Kaden Phillip Ackerman sit down," Rebecca ordered.

Marshall leaned toward the boy and whispered loudly, "Don't go anywhere near that girl. She'll give you the virus."

I cleared my throat. "That's not how the transmission works—"

Liam interrupted me. "The Z-virus is only contagious after death, right Doc?" He handed me my messenger bag.

Technically, yes. I nodded and slung the strap around my shoulder. The infected person had twenty-four hours before the virus killed and reanimated them. If Havana was correct on the time of Mira's infection, the girl had roughly ten more hours to live.

"Kaden, you can see Mira when she's all better," Havana said in a calm voice. Her unshakable faith in my abilities splintered my heart.

Getting ahold of myself, I checked that the prescription sedative I'd found in one of the hotel rooms was still inside the bag. Mentally, I calculated the dosage I'd need to stop the little girl's respiratory and circulatory functions.

Ah, Christ. My hands shook for a moment, until I brought my emotions back under control.

"There's no cure for the zombie virus," Marshall shouted.

Rebecca glared at him. "Shut up, Marshall." Then she looked at my mate with wide eyes. "Havana, were you infected?"

Havana nodded. "I got zombie blood in a cut right here." She held up her hand. "I would have died, but Mason healed me." Her eyes shown as she looked over at me.

"Are you saying there's a cure?" asked a blonde woman named Rhonda.

My mouth dried as over a dozen pairs of eyes focused on me. "I—"

Gabriel saved me by stalking over with a handful of clothes in his hand. "I found Mira's things."

As Havana helped the little girl put her clothes on over the much too large swimsuit, Nathan gave the Enforcers their orders. "Liam, you'll stay here and guard the hu—the others. Gabriel you're with us."

Gabriel and Liam nodded as if they'd been following Nathan's orders for a lifetime instead of an hour.

Nathan scooped the fully dressed Mira into his arms and we hurried to the lodge next door.

After a quick pit stop to pick up some crayons, we headed to the clinic. It was on the second floor between some offices and the stairs. The room was barely big enough for two exam tables, a desk, and a sink, but that didn't stop Nathan, Gabriel, and Havana from cramming into the dimly lit space.

As Nathan gently laid Mira on one of the tables, I went over to the sole window and retracted the mini-blinds. Bright morning sunlight streamed in, illuminating the room, and the stark expressions on Nathan and Havana's faces.

"What's the plan, Wheeler?" Nathan demanded.

Havana gave him a cross look. "*Dr. James* needs to examine her. Give him a minute."

The three adults moved back allowing me to stand next to Mira.

Although I'd already seen everything I needed to see, I grabbed the stethoscope and sphygmomanometer hanging on the wall and took Mira's vitals. Her readings were perfect. It seemed improbable that in less than twelve hours the child would be dead, but that's what made this virus so tragic.

Nathan watched every movement I made with an intensity that put my hair on end.

The Alpha was barely keeping it together. I feared how he'd react when he discovered the reality of the situation.

"Can I look at this?" Mira asked, pointing at the stethoscope. There was no resisting the impish grin on her face.

"Be careful," I said, handing it to her. Medical equipment would be hard to come by in future days.

Nathan rounded on me. "Can you save my child?"

I waved him and the others over to the desk so that Mira couldn't overhear us.

"Can you save her?" Nathan asked again.

I slowly shook my head.

Havana gasped. "But you saved me. Why can't you save Mira?"

"I used Tasha's blood to push you through your first transition. Mira is nowhere near her transition. If she could shift she could heal herself, but she can't so—"

"She'll die," Nathan finished. He looked at his daughter, the color leeching from his face.

"No. That can't happen. It can't be..." Havana's legs gave out.

Gabriel caught her before she collapsed.

Feeling her pain and grief as keenly as my own, I wheeled the desk chair around and helped Gabriel situate her on it.

Havana white-knuckled the chair armrests. "We can at least try giving her Tasha's blood."

"I'll go to Sanctuary and get some," Gabriel announced, heading toward the door.

I held up my hand to stop him. "We don't have any more of Tasha's blood." Liam had brought all the Beast's blood bags to the cabin when we were trying to save Havana's life. The ones we hadn't transfused into Havana were long destroyed.

Nathan balled his hands into fists. "If it will cure my baby, then I'll go to the Beast and drain her dry."

Gabriel snorted. "Even if you could somehow get Tasha's blood, you'd never get from here to Winterhaven and back in time."

Nathan's expression fell.

Havana wrung her hands. "What makes Tasha's blood so special? Can't you just use our blood?"

"It's not that simple." I ran my hands through my hair. "I've been searching for a cure to the Z-virus for weeks. I've analyzed every sample of Lykos blood I could get my hands on and all were effective at killing the Z-virus—"

Havana opened her mouth.

I continued before she could say anything. "—along with all other healthy cells. Just a small amount of Lykos blood is fatal to human and latents."

Gabriel nodded his head. "Everyone knows that, Mason."

"I didn't know that," Havana said in a small voice.

I gentled my tone and took her hand. "For some unknown reason, Tasha's blood helped heal you without killing you. I believe you would have perished with a transfusion of any other Lykos's blood."

"Do you think it is because Tasha is an Original?" Nathan asked.

I shrugged. "I don't know, but that's my prevailing theory."

Gabriel looked as if he was mulling something over. "Would pregnancy influence blood?"

Strange question. I looked down at Havana. "Well, potentially. The Lykos immune system, like the human immune system, is naturally suppressed during pregnancy to keep the mother from rejecting the fetus. Why do you ask?"

"Tasha donated that blood a month ago, just before she lost her last babe," he said slowly. "I remember it because she pulled one of my Enforcers off his detail to deliver the blood to Sanctuary."

"Tasha was pregnant?" Nathan asked, a look of surprise on his face.

"Yes," Gabriel said in a clipped voice, his gaze averted. "She had to shift to stop an assassination attempt at the Interfaction Games. She lost the babe soon after."

"That's terrible." Havana rubbed her still flat belly, her lips pinched together.

Hmm. Pregnancy was a unique immunological state wherein natural killer cells, immune cells, regulatory T cells, and neutrophils all behaved differently. It made perfect sense that the immune-system suppression of pregnancy would mute the normally lethal aspects of our blood. Otherwise, the Lykos species would have died generations ago. "You may be on to something, Gabriel."

I looked from Havana to Mira, my mind bubbling with possibilities. "We may have our cure."

Nathan's gaze fixed on my face. "We do?"

"We do?" Havana echoed, her full lips falling open in surprise. "What is it?"

I leaned down and kissed her nose. "It's sitting in front of me."

8

HAVANA

Keeping my head turned from the doctor drawing blood out of my arm, I focused on the little girl coloring pictures on the exam paper. *Please let my blood heal Mira.* The alternative was far too painful to consider. My throat grew tight and tears stung my eyes.

Mason, always sensitive to my moods, paused. "Are you okay, love?"

"Yes." *No.* If I'd only rescued her from the helicopter sooner, she never would have been infected. Even worse, some part of me must've known about the virus. *That's why I've been feeling dread this whole time.*

Gabriel squeezed my free hand. "Don't you dare blame yourself, Princess. The fault is mine for not getting the chopper in the air fast enough."

Nathan, who held his hand down on the exam table for Mira to outline, looked over at Gabriel. "No. The fault is mine for putting Mira in that situation."

Mira stopped coloring and cocked her head to the side. "What's a sit chew shon?" While her father murmured a reply, her gaze fell on the syringe in my arm. "Does that hurt?" She tried to jump off the table.

Nathan caught her before she reached us. "Sunshine, you need to sit there." His voice was steady and without the panicked pitch it'd held just minutes ago. He too held onto hope that my blood would help Mira.

Please let this cure her. A fist seemed to close around my heart and I struggled to take a breath.

"Are you sure you're okay, love?" Mason asked, switching out another test tube.

I nodded. "Do we have to worry about our blood types being incompatible?" I didn't even know what my blood type was.

Mason shook his head. "That would be the least of our concern." He switched the full test tube with another one.

"Enough." Gabriel stepped closer to the desk. "You've taken five vials already. Havana won't have any blood left in her body."

Mason let out a strained laugh. "It looks like more than it is. I want to be sure we have enough." He untied the elastic tourniquet on my upper arm.

"Take whatever you need." I'd give anything to keep Mira alive.

Nathan looked over at me. *"Thank you."* His gratitude and appreciation poured through our bond.

"Don't thank me, yet," I cautioned. *"We don't know if this will work."*

"I think it will work," Mason said, insinuating himself into our conversation.

Instead of being angry at the intrusion, Nathan gave the doctor a grateful look. "When will you give her the infusion?"

"In just a minute." Mason popped out the last vial and removed the needle from my arm. "Gabriel, make yourself useful and hold this down." He pushed Gabriel's finger over a cotton ball on the inside of my elbow and brought the vials of blood over to the windowsill. With careful precision he lined them up.

Gabriel pressed down on my arm with enough force to make my eyes water.

"Easy there." I pulled my arm away.

"Did I hurt you? I'm sorry." The huge male crouched down next to my chair and kissed my arm.

The move was so uncharacteristic for him, I smiled. "I think that's the first time I've ever heard you apologize for anything. You never said sorry for being such a dick to me when we first met."

Gabriel wrapped his arms around me and laid his head in my lap. "I'm sorry you thought I was a dick."

I yanked his hair.

He yelped and nipped at my thigh through the fabric of the robe. "I'm sorry I was rude. But didn't I make it up to you by giving you a babe?" He rested his hand on my stomach.

"How do you know you're the father?" I asked, amused by his arrogance.

"I just do," he said with a cocky grin.

"Do you have children with anyone else?" I asked, not liking the idea.

"No," he said quickly. "I've never wanted young before. Not until I met you."

I rubbed the black stubble on his chin trying to imagine a child with his bronze skin, dark hair, and flashing eyes. "Your daughter would be breathtaking."

"Our sons would be invincible," he corrected.

Liam's deep voice rang in my mind. *"Is everything okay?"*

Gabriel must've been on the telepathic channel too, because he responded, *"We don't know yet, broth—"*

"Stop!" Nathan shouted at Mason who'd approached Mira with a blood-filled syringe.

Gabriel jumped to his feet, looking ready to attack something.

I tried to stand, but my spinning head had me sitting back down. "What's wrong, Nathan?"

The Alpha male looked over Mason's shoulder at me. "What if this injection—"

"Infusion," Mason corrected.

Nathan thrust his hands through his hair. "What if this infusion doesn't work? What will happen?"

Mason must have responded telepathically, because Nathan rocked back on his heels. "No," he murmured.

I looked between them, quickly filling in the blanks. *Oh, God. The blood could kill her.*

Mason spun around to look at me. *"The blood is the only thing that may save her."*

May being the operative word. My hands shook as I twisted the belt of my robe into knots. "Could we test it first?"

"I'll get a human," Gabriel announced, moving toward the door.

"No!" I yelled. "We can't use the survivors as guinea pigs."

Mason nodded. "Agreed."

"Why not?" Gabriel asked.

"I can't believe you would even ask that," I replied, shocked by his utter lack of morality.

"You're the one who suggested we test it," Gabriel countered.

He's right. The guy who used to assassinate people isn't expected to have a conscience, but I should. Swamped in shame, I looked over at Nathan.

He wore a conflicted expression as if he too was struggling with the idea of risking another's life to save Mira.

"I won't entertain the notion of infusing a healthy person," Mason said with a quick shake of his head. "The only reason I'm trialing this on Mira is if it doesn't work, she'll be no worse off."

Translation, she'd be dead. I blinked furiously to keep my tears from falling.

"Lykos blood poisoning is a painful way to go," Gabriel added with a grimace.

I sucked in a breath. "It is?" *Oh, God, maybe we should rethink this.*

Mason gave the dark-haired male a sharp look. "In that event, this will make her passing quick and painless." He motioned down at a syringe filled with cloudy white fluid.

Although Nathan didn't visibly react to Mason's words, our bond exploded with grief and pain.

Needing to comfort him, I used the desk to push myself to my feet. This time, after an initial spell of dizziness, I stayed upright.

Gabriel reached for my arm, but I gently pushed him away. I needed to be with Mira and Nathan. Slowly I made my way over to them.

Nathan was staring down at his daughter, tears welling in his eyes. "I need a minute," he said in a choked voice.

"Why is Daddy crying?" Mira asked me.

I sat down next to her on the table and put my arm around her. "He's just worried about you. We all are."

She burrowed into my lap. "I'm worried too."

"There's no reason to be." I tried to keep my voice comforting.

"But he'll stab me with that." She peeked around my arm at Mason who waited with the syringe.

I smoothed back a tendril of her hair. "It's only a pinch, love bug. Look my arm has already healed." I showed her the inside of my elbow.

She didn't look convinced.

I glanced at Nathan.

Shirtless, barefoot, his gaunt face wracked with indecision and grief, the Alpha male had never looked less like the dominating billionaire, businessman, who'd swept me off my feet.

"Honey, what do you want to do?" I asked gently.

Nathan's ran his hand through his silver-streaked hair. *"I don't know. Damn the fates. I don't fucking know. What do you think we should do?"*

I blinked in surprise. Nathan was always decisive and sure of himself. Never once had he consulted me on a single decision, even when ordering food from a restaurant. It was an aspect of his personality that both intrigued me and drove me crazy. Seeing this vulnerable side of him tugged at my heart.

I glanced at Mason. *"Can we wait on giving Mira the cure?"*

The doctor frowned. *"We can. However, every second we delay the virus damages more vital organs. Acting sooner versus later may increase the odds of a positive outcome."*

That settles it. I took a deep breath, inhaling Mira's little girl smell, imprinting it to memory. "Can you be brave?" I asked her, but my gaze was on Nathan.

"Yes," she said, her face muffled against my side.

Nathan gave a small jerk of his head. He walked over to the table and wrapped his arms around the two of us. "I love you so much."

The tears running down his face mingled with the tears running down mine.

I sobbed and clung to them both. *"Nathan, we can't lose her."*

Nathan tightened his grip around us. *"We won't."* It was the promise of a desperate man, but it was comforting just the same.

"Daddy, you're messing up my hairloom!" Mira squeaked.

Nathan let out a weak laugh and pulled away. "You're my little miracle you know that?" He tapped the diamond hairpiece.

"I know," she said with a smile that would break hearts one day. "Okay, I can be brave." She held out her arm.

Mason had me grip the underside of her elbow to keep it extended, while he slowly injected my blood into her vein.

Other than a small flinch at the insertion of the needle, Mira held herself still.

"I'm so proud of you," I exclaimed as Mason withdrew the needle and put a Band-Aid over the tiny puncture. I leaned over to kiss her cheek. The sight of black veins crawling up her chin made me gasp.

Nathan cursed. "The virus is spreading."

Mason, who'd been putting the syringe into a sharps container, pushed Nathan aside and peered at Mira's face and neck. The serious expression he wore sent a chill down my spine.

Mira let out a heart-wrenching cry and convulsed in my arms.

"What's happening?" I cried, trying to keep a grip on her thrashing body.

"Mira!" Nathan shouted, pulling her from me.

Mira's eyes rolled back as her entire body trembled and shook.

"It's okay, sunshine," Nathan chanted, rocking her body.

Oh, God! Helplessness and raw terror engulfed me.

"Lay her on the floor!" Mason ordered.

As Nathan eased her shaking body down, Mason turned Mira on her side and slid a ball of fabric under her head.

If anything Mira shook more violently, blood trickling from her mouth and nose. The sound of her bones snapping shredded my soul.

Nathan let out a choking sound. "I'm here, sunshine. Daddy is right here." He lifted his tear-covered face to Mason and yelled, "Fucking do something. Don't let my baby suffer."

Mason reached for the syringe with the cloudy liquid.

No. No. No. A piercing scream ripped from my lips. "Mira!"

"Get Havana out!" Mason shouted to Gabriel.

Moving in a blur, Gabriel rushed across the room, hauled me into his arms and carried me out.

I fought him, scratching, and kicking the entire way.

When he finally set me on the wooden bench outside the door, blood streaked down his face.

Wracked with grief, I didn't care that I'd injured him. "I need to see her. Let me go back in there!"

Gabriel braced his arms around me, refusing to let me up. "There's nothing to see in there but death."

An unbearable wave of sorrow consumed me, leaving me sobbing and clinging to Gabriel as if he were my lifeline.

Liam reached out to us. *"What's happening?"*

"Not now, brother," Gabriel said, wrapping his arms around me.

"How can this happen?" Mira was so young. Sassy and sweet. Stubborn and charming. She loved dressing up and hated eating vegetables. A deep and searing anger stirred inside me. "It's not fair."

"No, it's not, Princess." Gabriel swiped his hand across his bloody face.

"I'm sorry." I let out a ragged breath and sagged against the wall.

Shouting from inside the clinic interrupted Gabriel's reply.

I stiffened. *What's happening now?*

Something thudded against the other side of the clinic door.

"Ah, fuck. The child must've reanimated." Gabriel stood and pulled a wicked-looking knife from the waistband of his jeans. "Wait here."

I grabbed his arm. "You don't know that! What if the cure

worked?" Hope and terror churned inside me as I stared at the shaking door.

"Stay back!" Gabriel pushed me behind him and turned the doorknob.

The door swung open and a huge wolf barreled straight at us.

❅ 9 ❅

GABRIEL

There was only a second to register sharp teeth and claws coming at my pregnant mate. *Threat!* Primal reflexes honed from decades of training, killing, and fighting for my life had me raising one arm out to protect Havana while I swung my knife into the attacking creature's side.

It let out a high-pitched yelp and fell to the ground.

"That's Mira!" shouted Nathan, rushing to the doorway. "You stabbed my daughter, motherfucker."

Havana let out a soft cry. "Oh, no!"

I looked down at the large wolf on the floor noting the silver-streaked fur. *Ah, fuck. What have I done?*

"She'll heal." *She has to heal.* I bent down and ripped the knife out of her side.

Mira let out a pain-filled yelp.

"*Brother!*" Liam mentally shouted in my mind. "*What's happening?*"

"*Not now, Liam!*" *Shit.* I didn't know Mira could shift, much less into an adult-sized wolf.

Havana shoved me aside and fell onto the ground next to

Mira. She was joined by Nathan who gathered his daughter's lupine body in his arms.

"I didn't know," I whispered. I never would have knowingly harmed the little Alpha. She reminded me so much of the girl my niece could have grown into.

I've killed Mira just like I killed Isla.

I stumbled back, nearly slipping on the wet floor. There was blood everywhere—pooling under the wolf's body, on Havana's robe, on the knife in my hand.

With a cry, I released the weapon. It hit the wood floor with a wet thunk.

The coppery scent of blood stung my nostrils and dragged me straight into the memory of that terrible night.

The plaintive wail of a babe rang in my mind. Horrific images followed. Me silencing Isla's newborn cries with my blade. Me cutting down my sister, her mate, my parents. Their anguished screams at my betrayal. My own silent scream as I tried desperately to fight Tasha's order to kill my family. I'd been helpless to resist Tasha's compulsion and unable to stop my body from turning on the people I loved.

Havana had helped me finally forgive myself for the atrocities I'd committed. She'd made me see Tasha's compulsion was entirely to blame. But I hadn't been under any compulsion when I struck down Mira just now.

Accident or not, I'd attacked and possibly killed another innocent babe. A chainsaw of guilt and shame ripped into me.

"Shift, sunshine," Nathan said in a commanding voice.

Mira's breathing became labored. Her eyes took on the glassiness of impending death.

Ah, fuck.

"My compulsion isn't working," Nathan cried, his eyes frantic with worry. He glared up at me. "If you killed my daughter, I will end you."

If another babe died by my hand, I deserved that and

more. I bowed my head willing to accept whatever punishment he dealt me.

"Where's Mason?" Havana cried. "He'd know what to do."

Nathan glanced back inside the clinic. "Mason's unconscious. You have to compel Mira. Don't let her die, Vana."

Havana took a deep breath and then shouted, "Mira shift right now!" Her voice thrummed with such power, my skull ached. "Mira, shift!"

Gripping my head in my hands, I shut my eyes against the pain.

The popping sounds of Mira's bones and joints remaking themselves was one of the best fucking sounds I'd heard in my life.

Havana made a startled noise.

"What in the fates?" murmured Nathan.

I opened my eyes to see Mira shift into the monstrous hybrid form. As she reared back on her hind legs, she lifted her massive head, and let out a roar that shook the wood beam ceiling.

Dust rained down on our heads.

What the fuck?

Stunned by the impossible sight and the ringing in my ears, I froze in place. In this form, Mira stood nearly eye-to-eye with me. She was the half wolf, half human killing machine only a rare few of our species could become.

Mira turned her bright gold gaze on me and bared razor-sharp fangs as long as my fingers.

Oh, shit. In this form, the child could easily tear me apart limb by limb. I sank into a defensive position, readying for her attack.

"Love bug, stop scaring Gabriel," Havana said in a firm voice. "Change back to human."

Mira tossed her snout from side to side and inched closer

to me. The knife-like claws on her paws scraped the floor as her steamy breath heated the air around my face.

From years of observing Tasha in this form, I knew if I ran or tried to attack the hybrid would take me down in a heartbeat. There was only one thing to do. I slowly sank to the floor and rested my head at her feet.

Mira shuffled back on her hind legs, seeming confused.

It's working.

"Mira, shift into a little girl." The compulsion in Havana's voice made my own head hurt.

Mira let out an annoyed snarl and slowly took her human form.

I blinked at her in shock and awe. Taking wolf form at her age was unheard of. Taking hybrid form should have been impossible.

"What are you doing?" Mira said, staring down at me.

I pushed myself up on my arms. "I was playing dead."

"Well, I don't like you." Mira stuck her tongue out at me.

Fair enough. "I'm sorry I stabbed you. I thought you were attacking Havana."

Mira looked back at my mate who was sitting on the floor next to a dazed looking Nathan. "I'd never attack Vana. She's going to be my mommy when Daddy gives her the sparkly ring." She whipped her head around to glare at me. "You can't come to the party."

Fuck me. I definitely wasn't scoring any points with the little female, but at least I hadn't ended her life. I let out a deep breath and picked up my knife from the floor. As I wiped the blade clean on my tattered jeans, I resolved to do a better job assessing potential threats before attacking them.

"Mira, come here," Havana said, raising her arms.

The little girl dove into them.

"The black veins are gone. You're healed!" Havana cried happy tears as she adjusted her robe to cover the child's naked body. "I'm so glad, you're okay, bug. We're all so happy." She elbowed Nathan.

The Alpha male picked his jaw off the floor. "Thank the fates. You gave me a scare, sunshine." He leaned over and kissed her forehead.

Mira smiled up at Nathan "I can turn into a doggie."

"Yes, you can," he said, a hint of awe in his voice.

"Can you turn into a doggie?"

Nathan slowly nodded. "All of us can."

But not all of us can take hybrid form. I looked over at my mate. When I'd seen Havana in hybrid form yesterday, I'd been astounded. Only Originals had ever been able to take the monstrous form. And now, with a dose of Havana's blood, Mira could transform too. It was incredible.

"Can Mason turn into a doggie?" Mira asked.

Havana twisted around to look into the clinic. "Mason!"

Nathan wrapped his arms around Havana and Mira. "He'll be fine once he wakes. I think he may have injected himself with some of that sedative."

Havana's eyes rounded. "Are you sure he's okay?"

"I'll check on him." I needed to do something helpful for a change. I stepped around Mira, Havana, and Nathan noting how happy they looked together.

Doubt crept into my mind. *Maybe Havana would be better off mated solely to Nathan.* Male-female couples were the norm in our species for a reason. Males, like me, were jealous sons of bitches that had a hard time sharing anything. Alpha males were even more territorial. Nathan and I would likely be at each other's throats for the rest of our lives. Lives that would be significantly shorter because Havana had claimed Mason, Liam and me.

Alphas lived for decades beyond Betas and Omegas, and no one even knew the lifespan of the Originals. They could be immortal.

Havana could be immortal. Or at least she might have been if she hadn't bonded to Mason, Liam, and me. *Fuck.* The realization that our bond made my mate vulnerable hit me like a punch to the gut.

Not wanting to examine those thoughts any longer, I took stock of the chaos inside the clinic. The desk lay on its side. The floor was covered in papers and medical supplies. One exam table had been overturned and Mason's loafers stuck out from under it.

Sighing, I maneuvered through the mess and hefted the exam table off Mason.

His chest rose and fell with a steady rhythm. Except for the growing bump on his head, he looked okay.

I was thinking about moving him to the hallway when I caught sight of the remaining vials of Havana's blood sitting by the windowsill.

If a dose of Havana's blood allowed Mira to take hybrid form, will it do the same for me? Would it make me an Alpha?

The idea excited the hell out of me. All my life I'd lived in the shadow of Alphas. Despite lacking the increased strength and the yellow eyes of the highest ranks of our species, I possessed their quickness and their dominant nature. It's what set me apart from the other warriors and made Tasha select me as her Head Enforcer. But it hadn't been enough to save my family.

I picked up one vial and rolled it in my palm. The red liquid swished and swirled inside like the fine wine I'd often seen Tasha drink.

Tasha's power came from her compulsion and her ability to take hybrid form. As the Beast, she could destroy anyone and anything in her path, but if we all could take hybrid form too, we could destroy her.

The thought had me clenching the glass vial. *I can avenge my family. I can avenge Isla.*

I pictured the beautiful face of my dead niece.

Pain and anger swelled inside me. Tasha needed to be destroyed. Nathan had a plan, but if he thought his political coup would work, he was kidding himself. The bitch would never concede her power to a bunch of lesser Alphas and council members. No matter how many other factions rose against her, she'd only fight harder.

Even after all those years with her, Nathan didn't understand the Alpha of Winterhaven. Tasha feared only one thing, those with more power. That was why she'd killed every Alpha female born in her faction. She took no chances that any female would grow in power to rival or exceed hers.

That's why we had to protect Havana and Mira from her. That's why we needed to do what no other assassins had done before—kill the Beast.

The idea of murdering a nearly immortal being would have been ridiculous just an hour ago. But now we had this. I lifted the vial, peering at the ruby liquid inside. *This can shift the odds in our favor.*

Determined to test my theory, I sifted through the crap on the floor until I found several packaged syringes. Not knowing what the different gauges meant, I tore one package open and plunged the needle into the vial.

"How is Mason?" Havana called out.

"He's fine. Enjoying a nap," I shouted back. I didn't want her looking in and trying to talk me out of my plan. If there was a chance her blood could change me the way it'd changed Mira, I had to try.

Once I'd filled the syringe, I lined it up with a vein in my arm.

"What are you doing, brother?" Liam's deep voice boomed from the doorway.

Startled, I nearly dropped the syringe.

"Since when do you do drugs?"

"Shut up and get over here."

Giving me a puzzled look, the giant waded through the mess. "Havana said Mira no longer has the virus. Good news. Right, brother?"

Aggravated with how long he was taking I clenched my teeth. "That's not even the best news."

"It isn't?" He ducked under a wood beam.

"Look at this." I help up the syringe.

Liam tripped over Mason's leg and nearly fell on the male. "Shit. Sorry, Doc."

"Never mind him." I waved my hand impatiently. "This is how we kill the Beast."

He squinted at the needle in my hand. "How do you figure?"

"After one dose of Havana's blood, Mira could take hybrid form." I snapped my finger against the needle.

A drop of blood flew into the air and landed on Liam's cheek. He wiped it off with the back of his hand. "You're kidding?"

I gave him a telepathic playback of the last half an hour. When I'd finished, his incredulous expression had changed into amazement. "I want an injection too."

I motioned over at the remaining vials. "Help yourself." I waited while he filled his own syringe with Havana's blood.

"Where do I stick it?" Liam tried to position his needle on the inside of his arm.

I shrugged. "How the fuck do I know? Just find a vein."

Together we inserted the needle into our arms.

"On three," I said. "One... two... three."

We depressed the syringe plungers at the same time.

Nothing happened.

Liam frowned. "Well, that was as anticlimactic as shit."

Disappointed, I pulled out the needle. "Maybe we need

more blood. We're a lot bigger than Mira." I headed for the windowsill where two more vials lay.

"Or maybe the blood infusion only works on latents," Liam countered.

I stopped in my tracks. *Fuck.* I hadn't thought about that. Still, I wasn't ready to give up hope just yet. "Let's at least try one more dose."

Liam suddenly groaned, his body shaking violently. "I don't feel so good." His eyes rolled back and he hit the floor.

"Brother!" I'd barely taken a step toward him when the most intense pain of my life hit me. *Fuck, this better be worth it,* I thought before collapsing.

❧ 10 ❧

HAVANA

If not for the persistent anxious feeling that hadn't gone away, I could almost relax.

Blissfully unaware of my worry, Mira slept in my lap.

I rested my hand on her back savoring her slow deep breaths. Those minutes when I'd thought she'd died had been the worst of my life.

Nathan placed his large, warm hand over mine. "Praise the fates, she's alive."

"Yes," I murmured.

Nathan went motionless, and then shook his head. "Screw the fates, you are the reason my daughter is alive." He laced his fingers through mine "Without your blood Mira would have died."

I tensed, uncomfortable with his gratitude.

"I will forever be indebted to you." His bright amber gaze glowed with emotion as he stared down at my face.

Okayyy. I was never one to look a gift horse in the mouth. If Nathan's appreciation meant he was no longer giving me the cold shoulder, I'd take it. "Does this mean you'll stay mated to me...permanently?"

He nodded.

"And you're okay with the baby." I held my breath.

He looked down at his daughter. "I love children."

"What about them?" I motioned into the clinic where three of my mates seemed to have disappeared. *What the heck are they doing in there?* Just a minute ago, there had been crashing noises. My bonds with Liam and Gabriel had flashed with pain, but both males had quickly called out that they were okay.

Nathan clenched his jaw. "We'll figure something out."

Filled with happiness, I leaned over and planted a kiss on his lips. "Thank you."

He deepened the kiss.

Sighing, I gave myself over to his masterful lips and tongue. No one could kiss like Nathan. It was as if he were seducing me and claiming ownership at the same time.

My head spun, and a moan escaped my lips.

Mira mumbled something in her sleep.

Oh, crap. Mira.

We froze and looked down at her.

Thankfully, she continued sleeping. Besides shifting for the first time, Nathan thought Mason might have injected her with some sedative before she attacked him.

Nathan let out a ragged breath and pressed his forehead against mine. "Damnation. I'm not a worthy enough male for you. You may not remember, but this is the second time you've saved my daughter's life."

I blinked. "What are you talking about?"

"When the housekeeper poisoned Mira, you knew just what to give my baby to make her throw up."

I stiffened. "Rachel poisoned Mira?"

He shook his head. "No. Mrs. Pierce did."

Ah. Anger spiked my blood. "I never liked that stuffy old bitch."

He chuckled. "Well you certainly gave her a skull thumping. Mrs. Pierce was in the hospital for a week after you clobbered her with a rolling pin."

I gasped. "I did not." Mrs. Pierce was practically a senior citizen.

"You did. But only in self-defense. You said she came at you with a knife. I felt so bad for ending your employment that day when I really should have been giving you a reward."

My head throbbed. I rubbed my temples trying to piece together my memories. "Why don't I remember any of that?"

He took a deep breath. "Because I compelled you not to."

"You compelled me?" I scooted away from him feeling betrayed. Somehow I hadn't thought Nathan would have stooped to messing with my mind.

"I only did it to protect you. At the time, I didn't know who had poisoned us and I thought you'd be safer if you didn't remember what happened and if you left us."

"But I wasn't safer, was I?" The memory of the rest of that night brought a bubble of hysterical laughter from my lips. "A serial killer kidnapped me."

"That was my fault." He clenched his jaw. "I'd compelled you to go straight home without thinking through my words. You left your car and tried to walk the fifteen miles to your apartment."

Realization dawned on me. "So that's why I walked home. You do not know how much grief Syd gave me for being so dumb."

Nathan looked away. "After that, Ty and I made a vow never to use compulsion on you again."

"Ty as in Tyberius? Mira's uncle?" I'd only had a couple run-ins with the dark-skinned model-gorgeous man, but he'd left an impression.

Nathan leaned back against the wall. "Well, Ty is technically Mira's brother since Tasha is his mother too. But we prefer to call him her uncle."

Brother. Uncle. Whatever. "When did Tyberius use compulsion on me?" I went over the few times I'd seen the mysterious guy before replaying the steamy threesome we'd had with him. My blood heated as I remembered how thrilling it'd been to be with him while Nathan watched. But Tyberius had abruptly walked out in the middle of our encounter and I hadn't seen him since.

Nathan pressed his lips together. "I, uh. Damnation. I don't know how to tell you this."

A sinking feeling settled in my gut. "Did you guys compel me to have sex with the two of you?"

Nathan's eyes widened. "No. We'd never do that."

"Then what?"

He rubbed the nape of his neck. "Initially, it was too dangerous for me to be seen with you—Tasha had her spies everywhere. However, I wanted to spend time with you, so I coerced Ty into dating you for me."

My mouth fell open. "What?"

"Ty and I formed a special bond when we were children. To survive Tasha's torture, we often retreated into each other's minds. It helped us cope."

"Okay," I said, trying to follow along.

"As a result, Ty and I can share each other's experiences. So when Ty took you on dates, I went along vicariously. I heard everything you said and experienced everything you did."

"That included sex," I said, trying to hide my inner freak out.

"Hell no. I made him swear not to touch you. However, sometimes you made that difficult." He gave me a scolding look. "You are a damn sexy female and when you put your mind to seducing a man..." He shook his head. "No wonder he fell in love with you."

I choked on my breath. *Holy crap. Tyberius loves me? How is that even possible?* "How long were Ty and I together?"

"You weren't together," Nathan corrected.

I wasn't buying that for a minute. "How long did you date me vicariously through him?"

He flushed. "Several months."

Several months? What the hell? Earlier in the year Syd had accused me of dating some gorgeous hotty with a fancy car. *Had that been Tyberius?* I closed my eyes trying to picture the gorgeous man in my mind.

A deep melodic voice whispered, *"You own my soul, Starfire."*

My head ached so badly, I let out a cry. "Why can't I remember?"

"Because I made him wipe your mind after every date." Nathan lowered his gaze as if he were ashamed. "I didn't know he was falling for you. I should have though. I was a selfish bastard." He tightened his fingers around mine.

I pulled my hand away. "Yes, you were." I couldn't even imagine what it'd be like to be with someone for months and not have them remember who I was. "So that's why he got weird and left that night the three of us were together?"

"I think it was too hard seeing you and I together." Nathan stared at the wall. "He shut me completely out after that night. I lost my brother because of my thoughtless actions."

I rubbed my chest not knowing how to respond. I felt confused and violated.

Nathan touched my cheek. "Can you forgive me for this too?"

I pulled away. "I don't know. God, Nathan, you make it so hard. You lied about your wife—Mira's mother. You broke up with me and shattered my heart—but that was supposedly all a lie. It sounds like you've repeatedly brainwashed me. And on top of all that you made your best friend date me and then made me forget him." I rubbed my head. "What else are you hiding from me?"

"Nothing. Absolutely nothing. I mean, there were a couple of incidents between us that I made you forget, but other than that, nothing."

"A couple of incidents?" Red crept into my line of vision. "Fuck you, Nathan." I'd had enough of his lies and the continual emotional roller coaster he put me on. First he loves me, then he doesn't, then he loves me, but not if I had other lovers, and now he loves me again. My eyes burned, but tears didn't fall. I was all out of tears for him.

"Havana, please you have to understand." Nathan tried to draw me closer.

I pushed him away. "I understand perfectly. Our relationship has always been about you and I'm tired of it." I gently shifted Mira's sleeping body to his lap and stood. "Nathan Steele, I unclaim—"

He grabbed my arm. "Don't. I beg of you, Vana. Don't do this. You're exhausted. You're upset—"

"I'm fucking furious." I gnashed my teeth wishing I could shift into my monster werewolf and throw him out the window.

"Don't unclaim me out of anger. Give me a chance to—"

"You're all out of chances. I don't want you as my mate any more."

He flinched. "Vana, please—"

"Don't talk to me!" I whisper-screamed.

The power I'd infused into my voice had him grabbing his head.

"I unclaim you, Nathan Steele."

As the bond between us snapped, he let out an anguished sound that echoed inside my heart.

The connection between us shattered, leaving nothing but a cold, empty space between us. My throat tightened. My eyes burned.

I desperately needed comfort from my mates. *Where were they?* I marched over to the clinic doorway and looked inside.

Mason lay on his side, sleeping peacefully on the cluttered floor, while Gabriel was trying to free Liam from inside the ceiling. Both males were at least half a foot taller than they'd been an hour ago and significantly more muscular.

I blinked, sure my eyes were playing tricks on me. "W-what the hell is going on?"

Gabriel looked over at me with bright golden eyes. "We injected ourselves with your blood."

I sucked in a breath. "You did what?"

"Your blood changed us both into Alphas. Now we won't shorten your lifespan." Gabriel grinned. "I think we'll be able to take hybrid form once I can get this big mother fucker free." He glared up at Liam. "Why the hell did you have to get stuck in the ceiling?"

"You're the one who wanted to ascend in this tiny room," Liam called out from inside the rafters.

"Shut up and duck that melon of yours down."

They were injecting my blood into their veins while I was going through one of the most emotional ordeals of my life? "Did you even consider telling me first?"

Gabriel frowned. "No. Why?"

Seriously? I ground my teeth together. "What if the injection killed you and by default me?" *And the baby.* I rubbed my stomach.

Gabriel gave an infuriating shrug. "It was a calculated risk. Besides now there is a far better chance we can make Nathan's plan work."

"What plan?"

Nathan gave me a beseeching look and opened his mouth. Nothing came out.

Oh yeah, I'd compelled him not to talk to me. *Good.* I didn't want to speak to the bastard ever again.

"Nathan's plan to kill Tasha," Liam called out.

"Overthrow," Nathan corrected. "We're only planning on overthrowing Tasha and you're not supposed to tell Vana."

They were keeping things from me now?

Gabriel snorted. "Fuck that. We'll kill the Beast. You should see how big Liam and I are."

Nathan let out a low growl. "I'm the Alpha, I say what the plan is."

Gabriel laughed. "Not anymore. I'm an Alpha now too and I can beat your ass six ways to Sunday."

"The fuck you can," Nathan said with an answering growl.

"I can break you both in half," Liam called out in a muffled voice.

"I can't believe you guys." Volcanic fury thrummed through my veins. These males were supposed to be my family. They were supposed to be the people I trusted most in the world. My heart pounded and my hands shook. I was so sick of the people I loved letting me down.

First there was my mom who rarely bothered to acknowledge my existence my entire life. Then the long string of lovers who cheated on me or broke my heart. And then there was Nathan... A vise tightened around my heart as I replayed all the times he'd hurt me. And now Gabriel and Liam who cared more about increasing their power than the potential risk to our baby. "Go to hell, all of you."

"Why is she upset?" Liam whispered.

"She's pregnant. It comes with the territory," Gabriel responded.

He didn't just throw down the pregnancy card, did he? "Fuck you. I'm leaving and don't think about following me."

Nathan set Mira aside and tried to reach for me. At the same time, Gabriel turned in my direction.

I raised my hand and called on my power. "All three of you stay here." I needed some time and distance from them before I did something I'd regret. Shaking with anger, I stormed out of the lodge.

Walking out into the bright sunshine did little to improve my mood.

"Assholes. I'm mated to a bunch of assholes." I kicked a pile of snow as I walked aimlessly along the path between the resort and the lodge. After two minutes of inhaling the fresh crisp mountain air, my anger slowly left me.

Gabriel's and Liam's decision to inject my blood without giving me a head's up was a dick move, but my reaction might have been a little over the top. And my decision to unclaim Nathan, although completely warranted, might have been hasty too. I ran a shaky hand over my face wishing I could undo the last hour.

"Havana? Is that you?" a voice called out.

I turned to see a figure running out of the ski resort.

As the person came closer, I recognized the heart-shaped face and wild cluster of tight blonde curls.

"Tina? What are you doing out here?" We'd left her and the two kids she'd been looking after at Sanctuary.

She ran over, her exhales fogging the cold air. "I'm so glad I found you." She threw her arms around me. The scent of blood and terror clung to her skin.

My adrenaline spiked. "What happened?"

"Come with me."

"Come where? Are the kids okay?"

She shook her head, her hazel eyes wide. There were bright red specks covering her face.

"Is that blood? Are you bleeding?"

Instead of answering, she grabbed my arm and started dragging me toward the parking lot. "Hurry. The kids."

I kept pace with her trying to get some answers. "Did something happen to the children?"

She didn't answer, but the anxiety coming off her spoke volumes.

The kids are in trouble. Even though I was still furious with my mates, I looked up at the ski lodge and mentally called out, *"Guys, Tina is here. She's frantic. I don't know what's going on."*

Liam and Gabriel shouted in my head at once.

"Stay where you are."

"We'll be right down."

"We're almost there." Tina motioned at a gold SUV idling a few yards away.

Where did she get the vehicle? I didn't remember seeing a car like that at Sanctuary. "Are the kids in there?" I tried to see through the darkly tinted windows.

"Hurry!" Tina screamed, tightening her grip around my arm.

My ears rang. "Lower your voice." *Crap, she's going to attract zombies.*

Tina dragged me to the passenger door. "The kids! We have to save the kids from her."

Her? Oh, God. I stopped in my tracks. "Do you mean Tasha?"

Tina nodded, her eyes filling with tears.

Oh, hell. "Tasha has the kids!" I telepathically shouted to my mates.

"Stop. We can't get to you!"

"Havana run back to us!"

Liam, Gabriel, and Nathan were hanging out the clinic window, frantic looks on their faces.

Why aren't they coming?

Tina whirled around. "I'm sorry."

The doors of the SUV opened and three huge guys dressed in black jumped out.

Crap. I turned to flee, but a heavily muscled, gray-haired male who looked somewhat familiar, grabbed me. "You're coming with us."

"Let me go!" I struggled to free myself from his hold. *Shit.* If only I could shift, I could take them out, but I couldn't risk the baby. Neither could I risk them taking me. Leaning into my attacker, I kicked him as hard as I could in the balls.

He doubled over, cursing.

Tearing free of his grasp, I darted around the other males. I'd almost made it to the edge of the parking lot when there was a loud pop and something struck me hard in the back.

Everything went dark.

TYBERIUS

There was a time when my mother's touch offered comfort not pain, when her lips crooned lullabies not curses, and when she gifted me with presents instead of near fatal wounds. But that had been a very long time ago.

Something rustled in the corner of my prison cell.

A mouse? A rat?

At this point either would be a tempting morsel. The guards hadn't fed me in over a week and the gnawing pain in my stomach destroyed any standards I had. Besides it wouldn't be the first time I resorted to eating vermin to survive. Once when I'd been a child, I'd survived off cockroaches for months. Of course, then I'd been able to make frequent escapes into my brother's mind to ease the despair of solitary confinement.

The silver helmet Mother had driven into my skull with spikes prevented me from even that small reprieve.

I tried again to reach Nathan telepathically. I had to warn him that the Beast had discovered our plot. My attempt failed like all the ones before. *Blast.* Mother had figured out that bands of silver around a Lykos's head negated most of their abilities including compulsion and telepathy.

Blast. If Nathan continued with his plan, he'd be walking right into a trap.

I didn't know who had betrayed us. It definitely hadn't been the Alphas of the Moon Valley or Red Canyon factions. Those poor females were locked in cells down the hall when Mother wasn't throwing them in front of me.

My refusal to mate with them, or any of the others, had resulted in multiple stab wounds and a castration experience that would live on in my nightmares for eternity. Thank the fates Mother allowed me to regenerate from that one, but she'd nailed the helmet back on before I could even think to send a message to Nathan.

"Nathan can you hear me?"

There was no answer.

Blast. Although we'd once been so close we could communicate over state lines, I couldn't reach him.

Biting back a moan of pain, I tugged futilely on the metal contraption that covered my entire head and most of my face. Mother had blinded me, but graciously left my mouth free, not that I'd ever say the words she wanted me to say. Never would I help her in her insane pursuit of more Alpha male children.

She'd fucked our childhood up. *Wasn't that enough?*

The scratching of tiny claws on the floor grabbed my attention.

Food.

I inhaled deeply, picking up a musty odor. *Definitely a rat.* Hopefully, a fat one. I tried to push myself off the cold slab of concrete. A torrent of pain clobbered me nearly senseless. Gasping, I closed my eyes.

Guess you get a free pass today, rat.

The most recent visit from Mother resulted in several

stab wounds and another broken leg. The injuries were enough to cause me intense agony but never enough to kill me. A pity really. I'd often wished she'd just put me out of my misery. But her torture always stopped short of death. Why she spared Nathan and me the violent ending she delivered everyone else was a mystery.

The scared and lonely little boy that still lived deep inside me insisted it was because she loved me. The realist I'd become knew the Beast wasn't capable of love.

As if to underscore my thoughts, the piteous moaning sounds from the cells down the hall increased. Mother had somehow put the Alpha females into heat and she'd left them in that desperate wanting state for weeks. I'd almost given in to the Beast's plan to give those females some relief, but loyalty to my beloved and the refusal to put any other babes' lives in Mother's hands held me back.

Still it was a constant struggle to ignore the powerful pheromones wafting through the bars of the cell. The scent left me hard and aching for my beloved.

Where is Havana? Is she safe?

I'd overheard the guards discussing the virus decimating the human population. They said humans were turning into the walking dead.

Havana needed me more than ever, assuming she was still alive.

That thought stopped my heart for a full second. If Havana died, I'd never forgive myself and I'd never forgive Mother for keeping me from saving her. It might be the one thing—the only thing—that would make me finally hate her. A line from one of Byron's poems flashed in my mind. *'The ruling principle of Hate, which for its pleasure doth create. The things it may annihilate.'*

Heavy footsteps thunked down the hall.

I tensed as they grew closer and stopped outside my cell.

The heavy metal door scraped open and a raspy voice called out, "Your mother wants to see you."

I wanted to croak a smart-ass reply to the male I'd dubbed, Guard Three, but my desiccated mouth couldn't form the words.

"Get up," snarled Guard Three. When I didn't move, he cursed, strode over and kicked my helmet.

The pain and ringing in my ears was almost worth his yelp of pain.

He clearly didn't appreciate my muffled laugh because his next kick landed near my stab wounds.

I must've blacked out from the pain, because the next thing I knew, I was being sprayed with freezing water. I shook my head, trying to clear it. "W-what's happening?"

Guard Three ignored me. He must've switched the pressure of the water, because it blasted me straight back against the wall.

Fuck. Somewhat glad for the helmet covering my head, I hunched into a ball. I'd forgotten all about the water cannon Mother kept in the dungeon. She loved to use it to reawaken her victims after they passed out. I guess I should've been glad they didn't use the boiling water setting. Having the flesh melted off my bones was always a fun time.

After a few minutes of spraying me down, the guard turned off the hose. "Dry off."

A towel landed in my lap. I tried to pick it up, but my hands shook too much.

Muttering several foul curses, Guard Three grabbed it and rubbed it across my body. Being half out of my mind with pain, the indignity of it all didn't shame me like it would have otherwise.

"What's taking so long, Keller?" another guard called out.

Keller, huh? I conscripted his name to memory so I could

find him later. Keller would pay for how he'd been treating those Alpha females and me.

"Don't use my fucking name, Ronnie," Keller shouted back. "Our Alpha wants him cleaned and dressed." He tossed a bundle at me. "Do I have to dress you too, you pitiful excuse of a male?"

I lifted my head and growled at him. It was a promise to exact an equal measure of pain.

"I wouldn't piss him off, Kell. He's her trueborn son," Ronnie warned.

Keller snorted. "If she cared for him, she wouldn't have left him here."

He had a point there. Blood loss, hunger, and pain had me dropping my cheek against the wet stone. It was suddenly too difficult to keep my eyes open.

Flitting in an out of consciousness, I was briefly aware of the guards forcing a robe on me and dragging me out of the dungeon. When I regained consciousness again, I sensed motion and heard an engine. *Where are they taking me?*

Oblivion dragged me under again and when I next came to, I was lying facedown on the pelt of some animal. The sound of a crackling fire and the smell of a burning hearth told me I was in one of Mother's receiving rooms. *Which one?*

I pricked my ears picking up a male's heavy breathing behind me. *A guard? One of Mother's Enforcers?* A quick sniff of the male's pungent body odor clarified Ronnie's identity, but his wasn't the only scent in the room.

The sweet scent of roses brought all my senses on alert.

Mother is here.

Blast. What did she want with me now?

"Stand, Tyberius," Mother called out. "I'm releasing you from your punishment.

Her soft tone put a shiver down my spine. *What's she planning?*

Long trained to hide any weakness from her, I tried to push myself to my feet. My arms trembled, and then gave out.

"Stand for your Alpha," Ronnie shouted. When I didn't react, he grabbed me and tried to force me to my feet.

A ferocious growl rumbled from across the room. "You dare lay hands on my son?"

"Apologies, my Alpha." Ronnie immediately dropped me.

I missed the pelt and hit the marble floor with a thud. *Blast. Why did Mother love marble so much?* If the helmet's spikes hadn't gouged out my eyes, I would've seen stars.

The soft whisper of silk announced Mother's approach.

I tensed, readying for whatever beating was coming next. *Whips this time? Electrodes? Hot pokers?*

She crouched down.

Although I couldn't see her face, I had no trouble imagining her visage. She looked no older than me with her long golden hair, shimmering yellow eyes, and tawny smooth-skin, but she was much, much older.

My robe must've gaped open, because I felt Mother's fingertips brush against my most recent injuries.

She let out a hissing noise. "Guard, did you stab my son?"

Is she joking or has her insanity finally taken hold of her memories?

"N-no," stuttered Ronnie.

"Who then?" Mother shouted.

Ronnie wisely didn't reply.

"Maybe this will loosen your tongue."

The soft squelch of a blade sinking into flesh was followed by Ronnie's shriek.

"Let's try again. Who abused my son?"

"K-Keller, one of the other guards," Ronnie cried. "Please, spare me."

Rookie mistake. Mother hated those who begged for mercy. The sound of several more blade strikes confirmed it.

After letting out a blood-curdling scream, Ronnie hit the floor. The area around me grew wet with his blood.

Parting is such sweet sorrow, Ronnie.

Mother reached out and patted my shoulder. "I will set this right my son." She raised her voice to someone else in the room. "James, find this guard Keller. Have him drawn and quartered. Then feed his raw flesh to the other guards. Let that serve as a warning."

"At once, my Alpha," James replied. "Also Zayn just radioed. They are at the Sanctuary gates."

Sanctuary? The mountain lodge. Why did she bring me here?

"Good." Mother snapped. "Did they locate the Alpha female Mason mentioned in his notes?"

"Affirmative. They found her at the ski resort. They are bringing her to you now."

"Excellent," Mother purred. "Tell them to be careful with her."

I cringed. That explained Mother's jubilant mood. She was hell bent on collecting Alpha females and forcing them into heat so she could breed them.

"My Alpha, Zayn confirmed sightings of Enforcers Perez and Murphy. They were most distressed to see the female taken."

"I'll just bet they were," Mother snarled.

"They also saw Ambassador Steele."

"Is that so," she said, her voice tightening. "Does he really think he can hide from me there?"

I tried to process their exchange. *Nathan is at the ski resort? Blast! He's too close. I have to warn him.*

"What about Mason?"

"They did not see him," James replied. "But there was a group of human survivors there too. Maybe he was providing them with medical—" The sound of a door opening interrupted him. He cleared his throat. "Here is Zayn with the female, my Alpha."

"Bring her closer," Mother ordered.

Heavy footsteps approached.

"She's unconscious," Mother said in an accusatory tone. "I told you not to harm her."

"We had to shoot her with a tranquilizer," Zayn's gravely voice responded. "She should be fine when she wakes up."

"She better be," Mother snarled. "If she dies, I'll hold you responsible."

Zayn swallowed audibly. "Can you tell if she is—?"

"She is. Not only that, she's about to go into heat again. Can't you scent it all over her?" Mother's laugh was a frightening thing. "Secure her in Nathan's suite and make sure she doesn't take these off." The sound of metal clinking made me wince in sympathy. No doubt Mother had shackled the poor female in silver bands.

"Yes, my Alpha," Zayn said quickly. "Do you want to send a team to bring back the others?"

"No. I have a feeling they'll all come to me," Mother said in a voice filled with dark promise.

Another male called out, "On our way back, we sighted a large horde of reanimated heading to the ski resort."

Mother laughed. "That should keep them busy for a while. Ambrose is it?"

"Yes, my Alpha." There was a nervous hitch to the male's voice. No one wanted to capture the interest of my mother.

"You and James bring my son upstairs to his room. See to his wounds and feed him, but don't remove his helmet."

My shoulders sagged as the hope I could finally message Nathan faded.

"Yes, my Alpha," the two Enforcers said in unison.

Mother clapped her hands together. "You have your orders, get to it."

Ambrose and James each grabbed one of my arms and hauled me to my feet.

"Oh, Zayn," Mother called out. "Havana is to be guarded twenty-four seven. No one goes in or out of her room."

Havana? She's the captured Alpha female?

A roaring in my ears blocked out anything else that was said. I sniffed the air. *There.* Through the heavy odor of blood and roses was the night blooming jasmine scent of my beloved.

The wolf inside me howled and raged desperate to get to Havana, but I couldn't summon the strength to move my broken body. As the Enforcers carried me upstairs, I vowed to save her even if it was the last thing I did.

❧ 12 ❧

HAVANA

I woke naked and disoriented, a bitter taste in my mouth. The soft sheets of my oversized king bed carried the scent of my mates, but I missed the crush of male chests against me. Moving my arm around, I blindly searched for a warm muscular body. When I didn't find a hairy chest or an arm, I cracked open one eye.

Crap. Too bright. I rubbed my throbbing head and grimaced against the early afternoon light streaming in from the large picture window by the bathroom. *Where are my mates?*

Since we'd gotten together, I'd never woken up without at least one of them cuddled next to me. It felt strange and wrong to be alone.

My aching head was slow in rebooting and I felt oddly drained for having just slept. It was only when I reached up to rub the kink out of my neck that I saw the silver bands on my forearms. "What the hell?"

The thick metal cuffs were a good two inches in width and looked similar to the ones Nathan had worn. *Nathan... I need to remember something about Nathan.*

I sat upright and paid for it with a wave of vertigo. Black

dots danced in my line of vision as the room spun around me. I grabbed my head, only to find a silver headband circling my entire skull. *What the hell is going on?*

"Good afternoon, my dear."

I started at the sight of a statuesque blonde sitting in the wingback chair next to the bed. Blinking hard to stop the dizziness, I tried to place the stunning blonde woman with glittering yellow eyes. When I did, my heart dropped.

"T-Tasha." *Oh fuck, Tasha!*

"Gabriel! Nathan! Liam!" I telepathically screamed for my mates, but my connection to them had vanished. *Why can't I reach them?*

Tasha leaned forward. The skintight satin dress she wore gaped open, making it clear she wore nothing underneath. "I'm the Alpha of Winterhaven. You may refer to me as mistress or my Alpha."

It'd be a cold day in hell before I did that. I sucked in a deep breath and tried desperately to piece together my memories.

"Since you've obviously been using this room—" she looked around the masculine bedroom her lips pinching together "—I thought you'd be comfortable here."

When I didn't reply, she approached the bed. "Normally, if I'd discovered another female using my home and my Enforcers, I'd carve them to pieces as slowly as possible and then, just before death, allow them to heal so I could burn them alive." The madness in her eyes made the hairs on the back of my neck stand on end. All this time I hadn't understood my mates' fear of this female. But I got it now.

Tasha's aura swirled with menace so dark and deep it seemed to suck all the energy and light out of the room. There was also an inhuman quality to her—the strange golden sheen to her skin, the way she stared without blinking, her predatory stillness. She was the scariest thing I'd ever encountered in my life and I'd gone toe-to-toe with serial killers and super zombies.

My internal warning lights were flashing. I'd been delusional to think I could take her on. Even if pregnancy hadn't prevented me from taking my monster werewolf form, I wouldn't wager a cent on me surviving a fight with this female. *How the hell did I end up here with her?*

As if I'd spoken out loud, Tasha said, "My Enforcers brought you to me."

Her words jogged my fragmented memories. "Your guys attacked me. They shot me with something." I rubbed the slight twinge in my shoulder.

"Tina!" I gasped remembering the frantic human woman. "What did your guys do to Tina?"

Tasha shrugged. "I didn't bother to ask. Maybe they killed her. Maybe they left her for the zombies to eat. Does it really matter? I'm much more concerned with you." She cocked her head to the side and studied me.

Some primitive survival instinct had me shrinking back from her. "What about the children? Where are the children Tina was caring for?"

"I haven't killed them yet if that's what you're asking. But I have fun plans for them."

"Please don't hurt them."

She pursed her lips. "You care for them?"

"Yes." I got the sinking sense that I'd been caught in a trap.

Tasha smiled too widely. "I'll allow them to live if you do everything I ask. Go against me and I'll use them as target practice." She pulled a long, thin knife from her thigh sheath and admired her reflection in the metal.

"W-what do you want me to do?"

"Just take care of that babe in your belly." Her eyes gleamed with an unholy light.

I scooted away. *How does she know I'm pregnant?*

Tasha chuckled. "I know all about the origins of the babe you carry. Mason was most detailed in the notes he left in the infirmary. It seems a transfusion of my blood turned you from a latent into an Alpha." She grabbed my chin and turned my face from side to side. "Fascinating. You have the look of your father."

"M-my father?" All my life I'd wondered about the identity of the soldier my mother had a one-night stand with. *How does she know who he is?*

Tasha made a tsking sound. "Zacharias always had a way with females. I'll have you know he was my first." Her lips softened, and she suddenly looked much younger.

I shuddered. The idea of my mystery dad screwing Nathan's psychotic ex was wrong on so many levels.

She tapped the knife against her lips. "Strange that one of his progeny should find their way to my door."

I didn't think it smart to remind her that her Enforcers had forcibly brought me here. From seeing my mates' memories, I knew she was capable of committing the most depraved and horrific acts imaginable. And now I was completely at her mercy. Shivering, I rubbed the silver band around my head.

Her gaze followed my movements. "The silver is a necessary evil, my dear. I can't have you trying to compel my Enforcers or warning your mates of their coming fate."

My pulse jumped. *What's she planning?*

She grimaced. "When I am through with those males, they will beg me for death."

Anger and fear had me blurting out, "Don't touch them!"

Her eyes flashed with rage. "Impertinent bitch." She slapped me so hard my vision went white.

As I lay dazed, she dragged her dress up to her hips and

climbed on top of me. "You're a pretty thing. I can almost see why my Enforcers betrayed me."

I shuddered as she ran her blade up my cheek.

Even if she hadn't pinned my arms down with her knees, I didn't dare fight her.

"Perhaps I should take one of your eyes for my collection." She brought the point of the blade under my left eye and pushed down.

The sharp bite of pain made me cry out.

The madwoman shook her head back and forth as if she were having some internal debate and then climbed off me. She took a deep breath and let it out. "You almost made me forget myself, whore. Don't anger me again." Her voice shook with enough power to make the glass window rattle.

I didn't feel a sliver of compulsion. *I'm more powerful than her.* Deciding it wasn't wise to let the psychopath see my cards, I lowered my head. "Yes, my Alpha."

She patted my leg and sheathed her knife. "Good. Behave and I'll treat you well. You'll have food, accommodations, and all the males you want to fuck. I remember how much I needed to mate during pregnancy."

She looked out the window and then back at me. "Mason wrote that he and my Enforcers weren't fucking you. Stupid males. I'll bet they didn't recognize that you're going into heat again."

I tensed. "I'm what?" *Is that why I've been so insatiable lately?*

"It happens sometimes. Usually a week after the first heat, another will hit. Twins are the usual result." She grinned. "This time you'll mate with an Alpha."

I have mated an Alpha. My heart wrenched as I remembered Nathan wasn't mine anymore and would never be again.

"You'll mate my son."

Tyberius? Funny that we were circling back to him again. I shook my head. "No. I've claimed my mates."

"They will never touch you again," Tasha spat. "Since you are soul bonded to them, I won't kill those worthless males. But they will atone for their crimes against me." She let out a chilling laugh.

Oh, God. I needed to figure a way out of here so I could warn them.

Tasha smiled. "Imagine how devastated they will be when they see you with my son."

I shook my head furiously. "I'd never do that."

"You will if you want the children downstairs to live."

Her warning hung heavy in the air between us.

I had to think of a way to protect the kids and myself.

"I do so like the look of that human boy. He's a feisty one. He reminds me of my consort at that age. Nathan always fought me. It made punishing him so much fun." She winked.

Bile rose in the back of my throat. I'd never be able to forget the memories Nathan carried of Tasha's abuse. "Please don't touch Isaac."

"I'll touch whoever I want." She clamped her hand around my ankle, her claw-like nails digging into my flesh. "And you, my dear, will fuck whoever I tell you to fuck."

The knock at the door saved me from having to respond.

Tasha moved so fast across the room she was a blur.

Holy crap. I thought Gabriel was fast.

Tasha yanked open the door and scowled down at an older woman holding a tray of food.

"You're late, Agnes."

"I'm sorry, my Alpha." The woman looked down at the floor, the tray trembling in her gnarled hands.

"Get back to the kitchen," Tasha yelled, snatching the tray. After slamming the door in Agnes's face, Tasha carried the tray to the bed and set it down in front of me. "Eat this. All of it."

I balked at the sight of a steak, hard-boiled egg, and a

glass of a thick red liquid I hoped was vegetable juice. "And if I can't?"

"Then that human girl downstairs will lose her right hand." Tasha tapped the knife strapped to her thigh.

I looked back at the food, my stomach churning.

Tasha closed her eyes and cocked her head as if telepathically speaking to someone. After a moment, she opened her eyes and looked at me. "My Enforcers are readying Tyberius. You two will make a beautiful Alpha male babe for me."

I shook my head. "Never."

"Oh, but you will, my dear. Fate has brought us together for a reason." She turned, walked to the door, but paused before opening it. "If you leave this bedroom or try to take off your silver bands, I'll break the human girl's spine one vertebra at a time. Little girls do scream so deliciously loud."

Her terrifying laugh stayed with me as she stepped out into the hallway and closed the door behind her.

✻ 13 ✻

LIAM

I sat in the hallway outside the ski lodge clinic wondering how this day got so fucked so fast. One minute I'd been soaring high on the adrenaline of having ascended into an Alpha male, and then I'd been forced to watch helplessly as my female was captured by Zayn.

The former Head Enforcer, known for his methodicalness and his absolute loyalty to Tasha, hadn't even spared Gabe and I a second glance before peeling out of the parking lot. No doubt he'd raced Havana straight to Tasha.

Why did they come for her? How do they even know about Havana?

I tried to focus on those questions instead of on the horrible fact that the Beast had Havana. Even worse, because of the compulsion Havana flung at us before she stormed out of the clinic, we couldn't attempt to rescue her.

After years of serving the Alpha of Winterhaven, I knew Tasha wouldn't kill Havana right away. *No.* The Beast would play with her first. She'd offer her some hope, and then snatch it away. Then she'd torture her—drinking in Havana's pain as she broke her body then her mind. Only then would

Tasha finally give Havana a drawn-out painful death. A death we would share because of our bond with her.

Fuck no. I would do anything to spare Havana that pain and agony, but there was nothing I could do. I'd failed my mate. I hadn't been there to fight for her or protect her, and now she'd pay the price. I wanted to howl my grief and frustration, but I kept it in. It would do no one any good. Besides Gabe and Nathan were already making enough noise inside the clinic.

The two of them had been arguing non-stop for the last hour, as every attempt they made to rouse Doc had failed.

They should just let the Omega sleep. At least then he could die peacefully instead of burdened with the knowledge his mate was suffering.

I rubbed my face in my hands, feeling the added length in my jaw. My face, like the rest of my body, had undergone a transformation. Besides gaining a pair of bright yellow eyes, I'd grown six inches in height and muscle. If I'd been a freak of nature before injecting myself with Havana's blood, now I was a monstrosity.

Why did I let Gabe talk me into doing the injection? Havana had been rightly pissed that we'd taken her blood. For all we knew the injection could have killed us all.

Ah, fuck. What does it matter now? We're all going to die anyway. I slammed the back of my head against the wall. It smashed through the wood paneling with a less than satisfying crunch.

A few yards away, Mira mumbled something and turned over in her sleep. Her father had bundled her in a blanket and only the tips of her tiny toes peeked out. At least the young Alpha female would survive. Discovering she'd been infected on my watch had disturbed me greatly.

Also disturbing, was the dead-eyed stare of the curly-haired human sitting on the bench across from me. Tina hadn't moved from that position since Nathan had compelled her to come inside.

She must be in shock.

When Nathan tried to find the source of the blood on her sweater, she shrieked loud enough to shake the lodge windows. None of us bothered with her after that. But maybe we should talk to her if only to confirm our suspicions.

I cleared my throat. "Tina, can you tell me what happened back at Sanctuary?"

She continued her staring war with the wall next to my face.

"Tina, were you attacked by a tall, blonde female, with yellow eyes?"

I probably imagined it, but the human's eyelids may have flickered.

"Did those males in the vehicle hurt you and the babes... the children?"

She blinked. "The children. The children." Tears welled in her eyes and she rocked back and forth.

Uncomfortable with her grief, I tried to steer the conversation toward the timeline of events. "When did Tasha and the Enforcers arrive?"

Tina gulped in a breath. "They came about an hour after Havana and the doctor left. Tasha attacked me..." Tina held a hand to her throat. "Those men with her found the kids and brought them to her. She said she'd hurt them if I didn't help her." Tears streamed down her cheeks. "She's a monster."

That's the truth. "Why did she send you and her Enforcers here?"

"To bring Havana back to Sanctuary."

So it was a targeted mission. Even though I'd suspected it, I still didn't understand. "How did she know about Havana?"

"I told her." Tina looked down at the floor, tears clinging to her thick eyelashes. "Tasha made me tell her everything that I'd seen at Sanctuary. I tried to hold some things back, but I couldn't. I couldn't stop myself from telling..."

"Don't beat yourself up." There was no way the human could've resisted Tasha's compulsion. It was a rarity than any Lykos could. "So Tasha wanted to take Havana to punish us all," I said more to myself than her.

Tina shook her head. "She wanted Havana because her men found the doctor's medical notes. The notes said Havana was pregnant. Tasha told me I had to help get Havana, otherwise she'd killed Isaac and Lily." Tina's lower lip quivered. "She really wouldn't do that, would she?"

A bellow from inside the clinic saved me from having to lie.

I jumped to my feet and nearly smacked my head on one of the wood beams. Ducking, I ran to the doorway.

Gabe and Nathan stood over Doc's contorting body.

I looked between the two males wondering why they didn't seem more concerned. "What's wrong with him?"

Gabe held up an empty syringe. "Since nothing else was working, I injected him with Havana's blood."

Doc seized on the floor, his muscles contracting violently. I didn't envy the pain I knew the male was experiencing. Those first few minutes after the injection were some of the most excruciating of my life.

"Get his clothes off." I shouted. Both Gabe and I had gotten tangled in our pants during our ascension. Not a fun experience.

Nathan and Gabe yanked off Doc's clothing and not a second too soon.

Golden fur erupted all over Mason's body as his jaw elongated and his limbs lengthened.

I expected Doc to change into his wolf as Gabe and I had done, but he grew larger and larger ultimately taking a half humanoid, half lupine form that took up almost the entire clinic.

Gabe and Nathan backed against the wall to make way for the hulking beast.

Gabe cursed. "Figures the Omega can take hybrid form."

Doc lifted his head and opened a pair of bright yellow eyes.

The three of us went motionless.

It can't be.

Nathan swallowed hard. "Is it just me, or does Mason look a hell of a lot like—"

Doc let out a hair-raising snarl that showcased his jagged fangs.

Fuck. I didn't want to experience the business end of those.

Gabe and Nathan inched closer to the wall, while Doc rolled onto paws as large as my SUV rims.

Although the golden-haired beast crouched onto the floor, his massive lupine head brushed against the sides of the hole my skull had punched in the ceiling. So much for me thinking I was the largest of our group. This version of Doc could break me like a matchstick.

"No one move a muscle," Nathan warned needlessly.

Doc's tufted ears went back, and he let out a low growl that shook the room. He didn't seem to recognize us. *Shit.*

I looked over at Gabe. "What's the plan?"

He turned to Nathan.

"Don't look at me, Enforcer. I told you this was a bad idea."

"Well, it woke Doc up," Gabe groused. "And now all of Havana's mates are Alphas so we won't shorten her lifespan."

"Like that really matters now," I couldn't help but saying. Alphas or not when Tasha killed Havana we'd all die with her.

"Look, Mason is changing back!"

Nathan was right. Doc slowly shrunk back into his human form, although like Gabe and me, he'd now climbed half a foot in height and muscle.

Doc looked down at his much bulkier body. "Bloody hell, what did you blighters do to me?"

"Not me, him." Nathan pointed at Gabe.

Gabe didn't back down from Mason's glare. "We couldn't wake you up."

"Yes, well, I fell on a syringe filled with a lethal dosage of sedative intended for Mira." His eyes widened and he looked around the room. "How is the child?"

I glanced behind me. "She's fine. Still sleeping."

"And she shows no trace of the virus?"

"No. Vana's blood completely cured her," Nathan said, looking both relieved and sad at the same time.

"And it gave both you and her the ability to take hybrid form," Gabe interjected, an envious look on his face. "It only gave Liam and me Alpha powers and it did jack shit for Nathan."

I blinked at the Ambassador surprised he'd injected himself.

Nathan gave me a quick look as if hearing my thoughts. "I had to see if it would increase my power enough to break the compulsion. Unfortunately, it did not."

Doc looked down at his arm. "You injected me with Havana's blood?"

"Yeah. There's one dose left." Gabe nodded toward the windowsill.

Doc's eyes lit up. "Incredible." He strode to the window and picked up the last syringe of blood. "We have a cure for the Z-virus." He grinned. "Does Havana know?"

When none of us said anything, Doc set the syringe down on the exam table. "Where is she?"

Nathan flinched. "Tasha has her."

Doc frowned. "That's not funny, mate."

"He's not joking." I hated how my voice rumbled through the room. It'd always been deep, but now it held a guttural pitch.

Doc closed his eyes. Then opened them. "I can't communicate with her. Our connection is dark."

Gabe cleared his throat. "Zayn shot her with a tranquilizer. She's likely still unconscious."

Doc's newly golden eyes blazed with anger. "How the hell did he get to her? Did you all just let him waltz in here and take her?"

Gabe and I shared an uncomfortable look.

Nathan rubbed the back of his head. "Vana was angry. She compelled us to remain here. She also unclaimed me."

Mason gaped at him while Gabriel and I looked away. Given the way Nathan had been behaving, he had no one but himself to blame. Still the male was in obvious pain and I felt bad for him.

"We're all trapped in the clinic," Gabe said, kicking at the medical supplies littering the floor. "We can't go after her."

Nathan gritted his teeth. "The Beast will torture her, and then kill her."

"That may not be the case." I filled them in on the conversation I'd had with Tina in the hallway.

Gabe scowled at Doc. "What the fuck? You were taking notes on Havana?"

Doc glared back at him. "Her transformation was a medical breakthrough for our species."

Gabe strode up to the now taller doctor. "You put our Alpha in danger, Omega."

"I'm not an Omega anymore." Doc shoved Gabe into the overturned exam table.

Righting himself, Gabe growled at Doc.

"Enough!" Nathan shouted. "This isn't helping Vana."

Even though Gabe, Doc, and I now towered over the Ambassador, the authority in his tone brought us all to attention.

Nathan cleared his throat. "Mason's notes may have saved Vana's life. Tasha craves an Alpha male son and as long as she thinks Vana might provide one, she'll want to keep her alive."

Gabe nodded slowly. "It gives us time to plan a rescue."

"Exactly." Nathan turned to Doc. "Did you mention anything about my relationship with Vana in your notes?"

Doc shook his head. "I mainly speculated on the properties of Tasha's blood."

"Good. Tasha has always been irrationally possessive of me." Nathan rubbed his hands together. "Our first order of business is to figure a way to break the compulsion keeping us here."

That would involve Havana canceling her order in person or us finding someone more powerful to override it. I wasn't optimistic on the chances of either of those two scenarios happening.

Doc looked thoughtful. "Since I wasn't conscious when Havana compelled you all. I don't think the compulsion would have worked on me."

"Try to leave," Nathan ordered. "But put some pants on first. My daughter is out in the hallway."

After struggling to squeeze into his now too small shirt and slacks, Doc waded through the mess on the floor toward me. When he caught sight of my face, his mouth dropped open. "Bloody hell, you're a regular behemoth now, aren't you?"

"Yeah, I guess so." Feeling like even more of a freak, I backed up into the hallway, allowing him to pass. "We haven't been able to get any farther than the bench." I pointed toward Tina.

The human slumped against the wall, her eyes closed.

"Is she okay?" Mason asked, a worried look on his face.

I shrugged.

Nathan appeared in the doorway. "First things first. See if you can leave this area."

I held my breath as Mason stepped past the bench and walked down to the end of the hallway.

"Praise the fates," Nathan breathed. "Go straight to Sanctuary—"

Gabe muscled him out of the doorway. "The sentries will capture him if he goes anywhere near the property."

Nathan sneered at him. "Then what do you suggest?"

In the corner, Mira sat up. "Daddy!"

Nathan walked over to her and picked her up. "Hi sunshine, how are you feeling?"

"Hungry," she answered rubbing her stomach. "Where's Vana?"

Nathan forced a smile. "At Sanctuary. Remember that big cabin in the woods I told you about."

Gabe and I exchanged a look. Sanctuary was more like a fortress. A likely heavily guarded fortress.

Mira pouted. "I want Vana."

"And you shall have her, Miss Mira," Doc said, walking back toward us. "I'm going to bring her back now." He shifted his gaze to Nathan. "I'll take the tram up to the summit. I remember it overlooked Sanctuary. I can get a bead on the situation from there."

"Can you talk to Gabe and Liam from that distance?" Nathan asked, waving his hands between us.

"No," Gabe and I answered for Doc. It took time and a deep bond to build that kind of mental connection.

Nathan rubbed the thick stubble on his chin. "We'll need radios then. There have to be radios around here."

"There are some in the ski patrol offices," Tina called out.

We all turned to look at the human I'd half forgotten was there.

Her cheeks flushed with color under our scrutiny. "I-I can show you."

"Thank you," Doc said. "Are you sure you're feeling up to it?"

Tina nodded. "I want to help Isaac and Lily. You'll bring them back too, right?"

"You have my word," Doc said in that smooth British way of his.

The two of them walked down the hallway, leaving the rest of us to worry and wait.

❦   14   ❦

TYBERIUS

"This is such bullshit, James. We've been pouring broth down Ty's throat for hours and he looks worse than he did before."

"We have to keep trying." James put another spoonful to my lips.

Feigning unconsciousness, I let the bone broth dribble down the side of my mouth.

"Fuck this shit," James shouted.

Something small and metal hit the wall with a clunk.

"He's too far gone," Ambrose said in a solemn tone. "The only way he'll be in any condition to mate is if he shifts."

"But Tasha said not to remove the helmet."

"Yes, but she also said to nurse her son back to health so he can mate that female tonight. Do you really want to inform the Beast that her son won't be able to perform? Because I sure as shit don't."

"She's off her rocker lately, not that she's ever been sane," James added in a low voice. "Abducting those Alpha females..."

"I heard every faction in the southwest has declared war on us," Ambrose whispered back.

"As if she cares."

"I also heard she's been killing all the latent Enforcers by injecting them with her blood. Isn't your nephew one of the latents?"

"Yes," James replied in a flat voice.

"Aren't you worried for him?"

"Of course I'm fucking worried about him, but my more immediate concern is what will happen to us if we can't get Ty on his feet."

I sensed both males staring down at me on the bed.

Take off my helmet.

Seeming to hear my unspoken plea, Ambrose said, "We'll take the helmet off and, once he shifts, put it right back on. Turn him around so his head is hanging off the bed."

Both males pushed me into position and took hold of the helmet.

Ah, fuck. This is going to hurt like a bitch.

"On three. One... Two... Three!"

A scream of anguish flew from my lips as the men ripped the helmet and the silver spikes from my skull. I took shallow gasps to keep from blacking out. Mother had really delivered on her punishment this time.

The Enforcers horrified silence spoke volumes.

"Damn the fates, she even gouged out his eyes."

"Her own son..."

I sensed Ambrose shaking his head.

"We have to get him to shift and then put this thing back on him."

My hands trembled. Never would I wear that contraption again. My inner wolf clawed to the surface desperate to heal my broken body.

"Look, his hands are shaking. He's starting to shift," James said, a hint of relief in his voice.

The transformation to wolf and back to human took far longer than planned, but when I was finally whole and healed again, I opened my eyes.

I was in my old bedroom at Sanctuary. Even though I hadn't been here in a year, the dark wood furnishings and heavy black curtains hanging over the windows hadn't changed a bit. The only additions included a larger television mounted on the wall and two Enforcers standing in front of my armoire.

James, a golden-haired, bearded male the size of a small tank, stood by Ambrose, an even taller, clean-shaven male whose dark skin tone contrasted starkly with his light-colored eyes.

I'd observed the two males for the past several years. Although both were strong warriors, neither had the power to rival mine.

Ambrose raised the helmet. "Don't trying anything Ty—"

I pushed every bit of my Alpha power into my voice. "You both are now under my command. Drop the helmet and don't move a muscle."

Ambrose dropped the cursed hunk of metal.

The oh-shit look on the Enforcers' faces was priceless. They'd been so concerned with what Tasha would do to them, they'd failed to consider what I could do to them.

Mother forbid anyone from compelling her Enforcers, but right now I didn't give a fuck about her rules. My beloved's life was in jeopardy. Holding the gazes of the males, I slowly pushed myself off the bed.

"Is Havana still here?"

The two Enforcers gave me blank looks.

"The female Zayn brought in," I said impatiently.

"Oh, her," James said. "Yes, she's down the hall in Nathan's room."

"Has she been tortured?" *If Mother hurt her…*

Ambrose shook his head.

I released a sigh of relief. "How many are guarding her?"

"Just one," James answered. "She pulled the others to help prepare for the council members' visit."

Blast. I'd forgotten about the New Year's Eve party. "When will the convoys arrive?"

"Not until the end of the week, but you know our Alpha."

Unfortunately, I did. *All too well.* Mother lived for the opportunity to showcase her wealth and power. It was no surprise she hadn't cancelled the event. Nothing impeded Mother's parties, not even the human apocalypse, wars with other factions, or discovering a political plot against her.

Which reminded me… I concentrated on the deep bond I shared with my brother. *"Nathan."*

I was rewarded with Nathan's voice in my head. *"Ty! Praise the fates. Where have you been?"*

"It's a long story. Are you still at the ski resort?"

I could feel his surprise through our bond. *"Yes. Enforcers took Vana—"*

"They brought her here to Sanctuary," I interjected. *"Tasha set her up in your old room."*

"Has the Beast harmed her?"

"I don't know." I looked over at the Enforcers. *"I haven't been able to see her yet."*

"Since Vana's mates are still alive, we know she still lives."

"Vana is mated?" And not to Nathan? That dumbfounded me for a moment.

"Yes," Nathan said, bitterness undercutting his tone. *"We're trying to figure a way to get to her —"*

Nathan couldn't come here. *"Tasha knows of your plot to force her out. Someone betrayed us, brother."*

Nathan cursed. *"Who—fuck, it doesn't matter. All that matters is saving Vana."*

"I know. I'm going to her right now. If she is able to travel, I'll sneak her out."

"How?"

I thought for a moment. *"Do you remember the tunnels we found when we were boys?"*

"Yes, but they became part of the underground bunker."

"Not all of them," I corrected. *"There's one that leads from the playroom to the south end of the property. Remember that time we escaped?"*

"Yes. Your mother nearly killed us in punishment. But surely, she filled it in. I can't imagine Tasha leaving an unsecured entry into her fortress."

"Either she forgot about it, or she deliberately left it as an escape route." I'd checked on the tunnel last year. As a spymaster my life often depended on knowing how to slip in and out of places unnoticed. "I'll take Havana through it. Can you meet us on the other side?"

"No, but I'll send Mason to meet you there. Keep me posted."

"I will." Our bond swelled with mutual regard. It felt good to have my brother back in my head.

"Who is he talking to?" James whispered to Ambrose.

"That's none of your concern," I snapped. "Which Enforcer is guarding Havana's door."

"Zayn," Ambrose answered.

Blast. The fierce Enforcer was one of the rare Lykos, like Nathan, who was resistant to compulsion. Even worse, his strength and fighting abilities were legendary. I doubted even the three of us could take him on. *Unless...*

I immediately rejected the idea of revealing my secret ability. It would be too dangerous. *There has to be another way.*

Thinking quickly, I said, "Tell Zayn my mother needs him

downstairs and that you will relieve him while he is away." Hopefully, the eldest Enforcer would buy that.

Ambrose and James nodded, and then headed out the door.

As soon as the males left, I collapsed back on the bed. Even though shifting had healed my injuries, the last two weeks of starvation and torture had drained much of my strength. With shaking hands, I picked up the bowl of broth soup and drank it down. It did little to fill my stomach, but I could eat more when Havana and I escaped this place.

Rolling to my feet, I grabbed the helmet off the floor. Although I wanted to hurl the cursed thing through the window, I carefully placed it on the bed and packed blankets around it. Not perfect, but it would look as if I were sleeping if someone merely swept their gaze over the bed.

Then I padded into the bathroom and washed the crusted blood off my face and head. As I gazed into the mirror barely recognizing my face, I rubbed the gold hoop in my ear. The reassuring sight of Havana's earring filled me with renewed strength. *I'm coming for you, Starfire.*

I considered dressing, but decided against it. I didn't need fabric getting in the way if I was forced to shift.

Deciding the Enforcers should have gotten rid of Zayn by now, I checked in with James. *"Is it clear?"*

"Yes."

I slowly cracked opened my bedroom door. The brightly lit hallway was jarring after the dimness of my room. My instinct was to stay in the soothing darkness, but that wasn't an option. With a quick glance out at the empty hallway, I headed toward Nathan's room.

James and Ambrose waited obediently by the door.

Ambrose gave me a hard look. "This is a bad idea, Ty. It's not too late to go back to your room—"

I raised my hand to stop him from talking. "Keep watch and alert me to anyone approaching."

Both males bowed their heads.

A husky moan came from inside the room.

The three of us stared at the door.

"Is she in there alone?"

James nodded. "Tasha told Zayn no one was to enter the room."

Another soft moan sounded.

Is she in pain?

Worry had me yanking open the door and stepping into my brother's old room. The intoxicating scent of my beloved drew my gaze straight to the large bed where Havana lay naked.

Her eyes were closed and her arms were shackled to the headboard above her. She tossed her head back and forth as if lost in a nightmare.

I scented no one else in the room. *Good.* I shut the door behind me, wanting to hide Havana's beauty from the Enforcers.

She was even more stunning than the last time I'd seen her. The fullness of her breasts and the cleft between her legs snared my attention.

Focus on rescuing her. I shook my head to clear it and rushed over to the bed.

Havana's eyes snapped open.

The sight of those bright gold irises stopped me in my tracks. *She's an Alpha. How the hell is she an Alpha?* I hadn't thought to ask Nathan when we'd spoken.

"Get away from me!" Havana shouted. "I won't have sex with you."

"Be quiet." I put my hand over her mouth.

She bit me.

Blast. I yanked my hand away from her sharp teeth. "I'm

trying to rescue you, Starfire. Remember me." I waited for the compulsion to bring back Havana's memories, but she only blinked at me.

She's more powerful than I am. My compulsion won't work on her. Shock glued me to the rug. *She won't ever be able to remember me. Remember us.* The realization destroyed a piece of my soul. *She's lost to me.*

As I stood there mourning the loss of my beloved, the fear in her eyes ebbed. She peered up at me as if trying to place me. "Tyberius?"

At least she remembered my name. "In the flesh," I replied, reaching over her to undo her restraints. Even if she never recalled our relationship, my memories and my love for her would endure this lifetime and any that came after.

Once free from the chains, she massaged her arms. "Thank you. Can you take these off too?" She tapped the band around her forehead and shook the silver cuffs on her wrists.

"I have nothing to cut them off, but we might find something in the playroom." I grabbed her hand to help her out of bed.

The moment our skin touched, Havana cried out. She fell back on the bed, her hand going between her legs. "It hurts. It hurts so bad. I need—ah, hell I need..."

She thrust her hips off the bed as she worked her fingers over her sex.

My mouth went dry and my mind blanked for a full second. Never had I witnessed a more mesmerizing sight than my beloved pleasuring herself. My shaft marbleized and throbbed painfully. *No. She's not mine. She's Nath—Wait she isn't Nathan's. She's mated to other males.* Males I had no loyalty to.

Havana moved frantically, rocking against her hand. "It's not working. I can't... I can't..."

I'd seen the same agonized expressions on the faces of the

Alpha females Mother had dragged to my cell. *What in the fuck had Mother given them to put them in this state?*

Seeming to get ahold of herself, Havana gasped for air and sat up. "I'm in heat again."

Ambrose's voice intruded. *"Zayn has spoken with Tasha. He's coming back upstairs and demands we explain ourselves."*

I grabbed one of Nathan's white undershirts from his dresser and handed it to Havana. "Put this on." I couldn't handle the thought of those Enforcers seeing her naked.

Once Havana had the shirt on, I scooped her up in my arms. "We have to go." I carried her out into the hall.

"Fight Zayn," I ordered the Enforcers. That should buy us a little time. Then I headed straight to Mother's room at the end of the hall. It was empty as I knew it'd be and the scent of roses was as suffocating as always.

"This is Tasha's room," Havana said through ragged breaths. Her gaze latched on to the life-sized portrait hung over the bed.

Mother always enjoyed looking at herself. "Indeed."

Havana rubbed herself against my bare chest.

I sucked in a breath deeply regretting the decision not to dress.

"I'm sorry," she moaned. "I can't seem to control myself."

"I have self-control enough for the both of us," I informed her and my raging erection.

"There's an elevator in her closet," she gasped. "It will take us to the lower level."

"We're not going downstairs." I carried her to the full-length mirror mounted on the wall across from the bed and pressed a small button on the back edge of the frame.

The mirror swung open revealing the hidden room behind it.

Havana's eyes went wide. "You're bringing me to a hidden sex dungeon?"

Rage filled determination had me racing as fast as I could down the ski lodge hallway. As soon as I passed the bench, my muscle locked in place and I crashed to the floor.

Fuck!

Liam, who sat near the clinic door holding the radio, shook his head. "Gabe, will you give it up already?"

"No." I'd never give up trying to get to Havana. My mate needed me now more than ever. I'd sworn to protect her. I'd sworn to fight for her. And now I could do neither. With a growl, I rolled to my feet and unsuccessfully tried to leave again.

"Why is the scary guy doing that, Daddy?" Mira asked as she played with the diamonds in "her hair.

Nathan, who sat next to her on the bench, rolled his eyes. "Because he's an idiot."

Out of respect for Mira, I resisted the urge to drag him into the clinic and beat his face bloody again. It was Nathan's fault we were all in this mess. If he hadn't angered our Alpha, she never would have trapped us here and run off.

Liam intruded on my thoughts. *"We share as much fault in this as Nathan. We shouldn't have taken Havana's blood without her permission."*

I hung my head. *"I know."* This was my fault. If I hadn't been so focused on growing my power and if I hadn't been so dismissive of Havana's thoughts and feelings, I wouldn't have driven my mate away. "I'm sorry."

Liam shook his head. *"Don't apologize to me. Apologize to our mate when you see her again."*

"If, we see her again," I corrected. The Beast of Winterhaven had never been one to restrain her murderous impulses. And nothing would rile Tasha more than finding a more powerful Alpha female. My gut told me that Tasha's need to destroy any possible rival would supersede her desire for Havana's babe. *The Beast will kill her.*

Ever the optimist, Liam said, *"Remember Havana is stronger than Tasha. All she needs is an opportunity to use her power—"*

"Which she will never get," I finished for him. Tasha took no chances. Moreover, the Beast's ability to foresee danger would eliminate any edge Havana may have had. I sighed and lay down on the floor. *"Face it, Liam. We are truly and royally fucked."*

Liam tapped the radio in his hand. *"We still have Mason out there."*

"The fucking Omega couldn't fight through a line at a supermarket. How the hell is he going to take down our brethren?" According to Mason's recent report, there were at least a hundred Enforcers at Sanctuary.

"Mason can turn into the hybrid and so can she," Liam nodded at the little Alpha female deep in conversation with her father. Static belched through the radio. Liam lifted it to his ear. "Mason? Anything new to report?"

I couldn't make out what Mason was saying, but based on Liam's frown, it didn't look too encouraging.

While my friend spoke to the doctor in a low voice, I looked over at Mira in puzzlement. *Why can she and Mason take hybrid form while Liam and I can't?* It made little sense. We'd all gotten the same amount of Havana's blood. Why did Mira and Mason have greater power? Liam and I, as trained warriors, should be stronger.

As if feeling my gaze, the small Alpha female looked over at me. "What are you doing now, scary guy?"

"Playing dead," I said, laying on my back and closing my eyes. Maybe if I feigned sleep the child would stop her incessant questions.

"We have to try again, sunshine," Nathan said to her. "Compel me to leave the ski lodge."

"Leave the ski lodge, Daddy!" the little alpha female shouted. Her words thrummed with enough power to make my head ache, but it wasn't close to the power we'd need to break Havana's compulsion.

If we couldn't break the compulsion, we stood no chance of rescuing our mate. Right now Tasha could be drawing and quartering Havana. Or boiling her alive. Or skinning her. Or breaking every bone in her body. "Fuck!" I opened my eyes and slammed my fist against the wood floor.

Nathan glared at me.

Mira looked at me with curious eyes. "What's a fuck?"

Nathan cleared his throat. "Nothing, sunshine. Why don't you look out the window and see if Tina is coming back with lunch?"

"Okay." Mira jumped off the bench and skipped to the window none of us could reach.

Nathan turned to me. "Watch your language around my daughter, Enforcer."

"Sorry," I said through gritted teeth. It seemed all I was doing today was apologizing.

Nathan ran a hand through his collar-length hair. "No, it's

me that needs to apologize. I'm sorry I've been hostile to you. If I'd been more accepting of your relationship with Vana, perhaps she wouldn't have unclaimed me." He rested his head against the wall. "Damn the fates. I all but begged her to unclaim me."

"Yeah, you did." Nathan might have been justifiable in his jealousy, but he was a fool to force Havana's hand like that. "Never give ultimatums unless you're prepared to lose."

"Vana was right to break our bond." Nathan sighed. "I've wronged her in so many ways. She's my chosen and instead of serving and protecting her, I've manipulated her and repeatedly put her in danger."

"You're not the only one." I thought of how I'd initially left Havana in a rundown cabin alone not knowing that she'd been infected. She'd nearly died because of my arrogance. As uncomfortable as it was to admit, Nathan and I were cut from a similar cloth.

Nathan cursed under his breath. "She deserves better than us."

I grunted in agreement.

Nathan continued, a wistful look on his face, "If only I could have another chance, I'd treat her the way she deserves. I'd serve her wishes—let her make the decisions. I'd accept any and all males she wanted to mate with... even you."

I bared my teeth. "Why, thank you."

"But I won't get another chance." Nathan closed his eyes.

Even though Nathan's domineering ways set my teeth on edge, I couldn't help feeling sorry for the male. "If we live through this, you can always win her back. She can claim you again." I really hoped she didn't though. With Nathan out of the picture, I might have a chance at being Head Mate.

"Once claimed, never put asunder," Nathan said, reciting the Lykos mating vows.

"That's bullshit," I scoffed. "My mother unclaimed and

reclaimed my father at least a dozen times." I would forever miss hearing them tell the tales of their tumultuous courtship.

Nathan sat up. "Do you think Havana might claim me again?"

I arched one eyebrow. "Are you worth reclaiming?"

"I see Tina!" Mira shouted, interrupting her father's reply. "She and Marshall are running away from the bad people."

"Bad people?" Nathan and I said at the same time.

"Yeah, the ones that walk like this." Mira staggered down the hallway.

Nathan inhaled sharply. "The reanimated?"

Mira nodded. "Lots and lots of them."

Nathan stood. "Damn the fates!"

I jumped up and dashed toward the clinic.

As I ran by, Liam looked up from his conversation with Mason. "What's going on?"

"I'll tell you in a second." I waded through all the crap on the clinic floor and stopped at the window overlooking the parking lot and the legions of zombies that filled it. "Ah, fucking hell."

There were hundreds of them slowly shuffling through the snow. The line of decaying bodies stretched as far back as I could see.

How did we miss this amassing outside?

"What is it?" Liam shouted from the doorway.

"It seems the fair citizens of Sunridge have come to call."

"The fuck you say?" Liam squeezed his gargantuan body through the door and crammed his way through the clinic to look out the window. When he caught sight of the army of death, he shuddered.

Mason's voice came from the radio clenched in the giant's hand. "There are ten Enforcers manning the front gates.

There have been a lot of incoming vehicles. Most of them filled with latent males."

Liam brought the radio to his lips. "Doc, I'll have to get back to you. We're being invaded by zombies."

"Bloody hell. Do you need me to head back?"

I grabbed the radio from Liam. "No. Mason, we need you watching Sanctuary. If you see any opportunity to get Havana out, you take it."

"But how are you going to deal with the reanimated if you're trapped in the clinic?" Mason asked.

The simple answer was, we couldn't. "We're on the second floor," I said to calm him down.

"But the human survivors aren't," Mason said, in a panicked voice.

"Give them some credit. They can take a flight of stairs." I snorted. "Keep us posted on what's happening at Sanctuary." I muted the radio.

Liam peered out the window. "There's got to be at least five hundred of those things out there. We're never getting out of here now."

I let out a dry laugh. "This just keeps getting better and better." I'd thought Havana would die and take us with her, but now we might be the ones to die first. "Either the reanimated will eat us or we'll starve to death in here."

Liam looked out at the ski resort. "And so will the humans. Fuck, brother. We can't let harm come to them."

As if summoned, one of the humans raced into the room. "Zombies! There are zombies everywhere."

Nathan strode in after him. "Marshall, calm down."

"How can I calm down? They'll kill us all!" Marshall's watery eyes were wild.

I considered snapping the annoying human's neck.

Reading my mind, Liam shook his head. "*Havana wouldn't like that, brother.*"

Fuck. Since I was already in the doghouse, I dropped my hands.

"Are the others okay? Sierra and her brothers?" Liam asked him.

"I don't know. That harridan, Rebecca, was ordering everyone upstairs," Marshall panted.

Nathan nodded. "Good. They'll be safe up there and there's plenty of food in the restaurant."

My stomach rumbled reminding me that we weren't so lucky. Trying to ignore my hunger, I concentrated on the agitated human. "Why did you come over here?"

Marshall licked his chapped lips. "You guys have the cure to the zombie virus, right?"

Liam, Nathan, and I exchanged a look.

Nathan stepped forward to grab the human's arm. "Not exactly, Marshall."

Marshall pulled away from the silver-haired male. "I saw your daughter out in the hallway. She's cured. I want the cure too."

"Have you been infected?" I reached for my knife, pleased to have a reason to eliminate the prick.

"No, but I want immunity in case I'm bitten." Marshall's gaze zeroed in on the last syringe of Havana's blood lying on the exam table where Mason had left it. "Is this it?"

"No," Nathan replied.

"Yes," Liam said at the same time.

"I knew it! You're trying to keep it for yourselves." Moving surprisingly fast for an old man, Marshall snatched the syringe and jabbed the needle into his arm.

"I wouldn't do that if I were you," I warned. We had no idea what Havana's blood would do to a human.

"Marshall, stop!" Nathan ordered.

But the old man had already emptied the syringe into his arm. He gave us a triumphant smile. "Now, I'm immune too."

His self-satisfied expression wavered after a second. "Ah! It burns." He collapsed, blood trickling from his eyes, ears and nose.

I cursed, recognizing the signs of Lykos blood poisoning.

Marshall let out several high-pitched shrieks, convulsed, and then went still.

The three of us stared at his dead body in silence.

Fuck. We'll have to clean that up.

Tina poked her head into the clinic. "What happened to him?"

"Nothing he didn't deserve," I said, stepping in front of Marshall's corpse. "I don't suppose you brought back food?"

Nathan gave me an incredulous look. "How can you be hungry after watching the man die?"

I shrugged.

Liam rubbed his stomach. "I'm hungry too."

Tina motioned behind her at the hallway. "I set the food out on the bench. Mira is already going to town on it."

The idea of a meal was helping to turn the shitastic day around.

Tina licked her lips nervously and held up a bag. "I also grabbed some explosives from ski patrol."

"Explosives?" I peered inside and was momentarily struck dumb at the sight of dozens of incendiary charges.

"Yeah, they have all kinds of bombs for avalanche control. I thought maybe we could use them on the zombies." Tina briefly met my gaze and looked away.

"We can toss them from the window," Liam said, his voice filled with excitement.

"Yes." I wasn't an expert in explosive weapons, but there was enough dynamite and ammonium nitrate to send our undead visitors back to hell. This definitely turned the day around. "I could kiss you right now, human."

Tina took a hasty step back making me regret having threatened to kill her the day before.

I gave the human who might just have saved our lives one of my rare smiles. Then, since I was on a roll, I apologized to her.

⚘   16   ⚘

HAVANA

My jaw fell open as Tyberius carried me into the best-outfitted BDSM room I'd ever seen.

The shiny white marble floors and walls contrasted starkly with the black leather spanking benches, sex chairs, and huge St. Andrew's cross on the far side of the room. Manacles hung from the top and bottom of the X-frame metal structure making it clear the device wasn't just for show.

Holy crap. This place was the real deal with medieval looking stockades and human-sized silver cages hanging from the ceiling. I peered up at the cages. "Does Tasha keep people up there?"

"No," Tyberius said, carrying me past shelves stocked with towels, riding crops, and whips.

Tearing my gaze from the line of mannequin heads covered with leather masks, I took in the massive prison cell that ran half the length of the warehouse-sized room. "Jesus. Tasha wasn't messing around with this place, was she?"

Tyberius set me down. "Mother calls this her playroom." The bitter tone in his voice spoke volumes.

I sought confirmation of what I already knew. "Tasha is your mother."

"Unfortunately." Tyberius swung his gaze around the room as if searching for something. His gold hoop earring caught the light from the sconces on the wall and winked at me.

Wondering why his earring looked so familiar I said, "And Nathan is?"

"My brother, in spirit if not blood. I'll get something to cut your bands off."

"Can't you just rip them apart?" I remembered how he'd torn off Nathan's silver cuffs during our threesome. The memory was enough to make another wave of sexual hunger whip through me.

"I'm too weak," Tyberius admitted.

As he knelt down and opened a black leather storage trunk, I studied the sharp planes of his handsome face taking in his hollow cheekbones.

He's lost weight. And not an insignificant amount given the broad muscles of his arms and shoulders were much leaner than before. I could even count his ribs and each one of his well-defined abs through his smooth caramel colored skin.

However, whatever starvation diet he'd been on hadn't affected his impressive cock. The sight of his thick, dark erection made my core cramp with need. A low moan escaped my lips.

He looked up from rummaging through instruments of torture. "Are you in pain?"

"No." *Yes. Hell.* I'd never needed my mates more. A spasm of desire hit me and I rubbed my nipples through Nathan's undershirt.

An answering flare of lust sparked in his eyes and his shaft throbbed. Despite his clear interest, he made no move toward me. "You've been drugged."

No shit. Tasha must have put something in my food that

increased my already out of control sex drive. Being in this room, surrounded by sex toys and bondage apparatus, was only adding fuel to the fire.

"Try to fight it," Tyberius said in a voice so low I wasn't sure if it was meant for him or me.

I stifled a moan as an insane urge to push him down on the floor and mount him gripped me.

Tyberius turned his attention back to the trunk.

Trying to get ahold of myself, I bit my lip. There was no way I'd fuck some random guy.

But he isn't a random guy, is he? He was Nathan's best friend. The guy he wanted us to have a threesome with. And apparently, the guy he coerced into dating me for months. "Nathan said you and I spent a lot of time together."

Tyberius made a noncommittal sound.

"Did we have sex?"

He jerked his head up and a pair of bolt cutters fell from his hands.

"So that's a yes?"

He slowly nodded. "It happened only one time... Nathan doesn't know."

Interesting. I guess he and Nathan didn't share *everything.* "Did you compel me?"

His golden eyes flashed with indignation. "No. If anything, you seduced me."

Hmm. Under normal circumstances, I'd be pissed as hell to find out I'd had sex with a virtual stranger who promptly wiped my mind. But the wave of feverish desire moving through my body made it impossible to think about anything but how sexy Tyberius looked. *I'll bet being with him was incredible.*

The gorgeous male picked up the bolt cutters and started cutting off my silver wrist cuffs.

"I don't remember any of our time together."

He stiffened.

"Can you give me the memories back?"

"No."

"Why not?" I was genuinely curious.

"Because I can no longer compel you." He tugged at the mangled silver at my right wrist.

The cuff fell to the floor with a heavy clink.

Immediately some of the drain on my energy stopped. I hadn't realized how much the silver cuffs had been sapping me. I tried to focus on how much better I felt instead of the burning need between my legs.

Tyberius closed his eyes and said nothing for nearly a minute.

Weirded out, I said, "What are you doing?"

He opened his eyes. "Talking to Nathan about you."

"Oh," I said feeling left out and strangely annoyed. "Could you talk to him out loud? So I could hear?"

He nodded as if my request wasn't ridiculous, which I know it was. Then he said, "I'm trying to get her cuffs off, brother. When I do, you can tell her yourself."

Curiosity got the better of me. "What does he want to tell me?"

"How sorry he is."

My heart ached. "Tell him that I'm sorry too." I never should have unclaimed him out of anger.

"She unclaimed you? Over me?" Tyberius glanced at me with a surprised expression on his face.

"That was one of many reasons." I frowned. "I did not appreciate the way you two repeatedly messed with my mind."

"No one will pay the price for that more than I," Tyberius muttered as he positioned the snub nose blades of the bolt cutter around the other wrist cuff.

I noticed how gentle his hands were on my arm. *Does he still have feelings for me?*

"No, Nathan. I can't compel her to remember me. She's too powerful now. It's done, okay. Let's focus on getting her out of here. Then she can claim you again after you apologize."

I stiffened. "What do you mean? Nathan said once the mating bond is broken it can never be remade."

Ty's brows shot up. "He said what?" A moment later he coughed. "Nathan says he may have exaggerated a bit in the spirit of negotiation." He pressed hard on the handles of the cutter and my wristband fell off.

More of my energy, along with my irritation with Nathan, came roaring back. "Tell him, that both he and his spirit of negotiation can go to hell."

Ty shook his head. "Brother, you keep digging yourself deeper and deeper." He tried unsuccessfully to insert the bold cutter blades around my silver headband. "I'm sorry, Starfire. I can't get this one."

I tried to hide my disappointment. "It's okay. We can get it off later."

Nathan must've said something to Tyberius, because his smile slipped away and he headed toward the back of the room where a bondage bed sat flush with the wall. "Come on, the escape tunnel is this way."

I tried not to be distracted by the sight of the sex swing hanging from the top rail of the bed. Locking my knees, I said, "No. I'm not leaving this place without Isaac and Lily."

Tyberius spun around. "Who?"

"The human children Tasha imprisoned here."

"If they're human they are already dead," he said in a solemn voice. "Mother despises humans for what they did to her when she was young." He shoved the bed away from the wall which was no small feat given the thing looked like it was made entirely of metal. Behind the bed was a brick wall. "Blast." Tyberius kicked the bed frame.

A voice I'd hoped never to hear again called out, "Has someone been a naughty boy?"

Tyberius and I froze.

A panicked expression crossed his face. "Fuck." He glanced back at the wall. "Nathan, the tunnel has been bricked over and Tasha is here."

I'm not sure what Nathan said to Tyberius, but the gorgeous male shoved the bed back against the wall. Then ushered me to the closest black leather spanking bench. "Get on this. Nathan says we have to make it look like I took you here for sex."

"Right." Since the alternative was likely certain death, being strapped down seemed the lesser of two evils. My heart thumped wildly as I climbed on the bench. There were leather pads for my stomach, arms, and legs. As I settled belly down onto the apparatus, Tyberius secured my limbs with thick straps and pushed Nathan's shirt to the center of my back.

"You know what I do to naughty boys, don't you, Tyberius?" Tasha said in a singsong voice that sounded much closer.

Fear washed down my spine as I tested the restraints. I was immobile with my legs spread open and my bare ass quivering in the air. Never had I felt more vulnerable and exposed and, since I'd been an exotic dancer, that was saying something. I counted my breaths, trying not to let panic overtake me.

"I'm sorry, but it has to look convincing." Tyberius brought his hand down on my ass.

The hard slap jolted me, scalding my skin. Shock gave way to desire as heat flooded my core. I let out a deep moan.

Despite the seriousness of the situation, my body craved the erotic attention.

Tyberius slapped me again.

The impact sent a lightning strike straight to my pussy. "More," I begged.

Tyberius obliged, spanking me again and again.

Each crack of his hand brought a mixture of pain and pleasure that made me shudder with want. My thighs shook as the ache in my pussy grew. I'd almost lost myself when Tasha strode into the room, a contingent of males behind her. They were all huge, muscular, and unfamiliar except for the gray-haired one I recognized from the resort parking lot.

Tasha caught sight of me on the bench and stopped. Her bright yellow eyes flashed with something that dropped my internal temperature thirty degrees. "Tyberius, explain yourself."

"What's to explain? I'm punishing my female." Tyberius gave me another blistering slap on the ass.

I let out a cry.

Tasha's gaze narrowed. "She isn't yours."

"She's mine," Tyberius said so fiercely, I almost believed him. "Never have I craved a female so. I want to mate her until neither of us can move." He gripped my hip so hard his fingers dug into my skin.

Taking my cue, I moaned, "Fuck me." I pushed my ass into the air. "Please."

He grabbed hold of my hair and yanked my head back. "So greedy for my cock, aren't you?"

"Yes, oh yes!" I cried.

Tasha looked over at the gray-haired male. "And you thought my son was trying to escape, Zayn." She let out a laugh that crawled across my skin like spiders.

Tyberius pinched my nipples through the shirt.

I swallowed back my shocked moan. "Ty, please." The nickname slipped from my lips, as if I'd been using it forever.

"I want to hear you scream." Ty slid his hands between my legs and rubbed my clit.

I shrieked at the intense sensation. "Please, Ty. Stop." I knew it was a ruse, but being aroused in front of his mother was degrading. Even worse, she watched every touch with that unblinking predatory stare of hers.

Tasha licked her lips. "I can help you punish her."

"No," Ty snarled. "She is mine and mine alone. I want privacy while I mate her."

"So possessive!" She sounded halfway between annoyed and delighted. "Alphas always are when they find their mates." She rubbed her hands together. "Normally I'd throw you back in the dungeon for compelling my Enforcers, but considering you're finally taking a female, I'll overlook your disobedience." She waved her hands at the males behind her. "Wait for them outside the room. When they are... finished, please escort them to his chambers, unless you'd rather she stay in a different room."

"She stays with me," Ty roared.

"Then it's settled." With those parting words she and her Enforcers left taking their menacing energy with them.

I dropped my head in relief.

Ty cursed. "Yes, I know we're alive, Nathan. But it doesn't look like we're getting out of here anytime soon. Oh, you've got a plan now. Care to share?" He looked over at me. "No. I will not ask Havana to do that."

I lifted my head. "Ask me what?"

"Nathan wants you to claim me because my mother would never allow me to die. Claiming me would keep you alive."

That made a kind of sick sense. "Okay."

"Okay?" Ty's mouth dropped. "You'd be willing to soul bond with me?"

I nodded. "Apart from the it-would-keep-me-alive-thing, you're incredibly sexy, and I must've thought pretty highly of you to date you." *And seduce you.* "Don't you want me to claim you?" Nathan seemed to think Ty was in love with me, but maybe he had the wrong idea.

Ty's Adam's apple jumped. "I do."

"Then I'll do it, but on one condition."

His expression shuttered. "What condition?"

I wiggled my ass. "You have to put your cock inside me." I know Mason told me not to have sex, but the need to mate burned through me with such savage intensity I couldn't think of anything else. Maybe if he just stuck it inside me for a minute, it would ease some of the agonizing pain between my legs.

"Are you sure you're okay with this, brother?" Ty asked the voice inside his head.

Screw Nathan. "Ty, kick Nathan out of your head and stick your cock inside me now!" My voice cracked as another spasm tore me apart. Every cell of my body begged for what only he could give me.

"I will never let my Starfire suffer."

I felt warmth at my back, and then his swollen shaft was pressing inside my slick entrance.

My eyes rolled back in my head. "Ah, yes. God, that feels so good. Fuck me a little please. Just a little."

He fed his cock in with slow pumps that took him deeper and deeper until he was completely buried inside me.

"Blast. You're so tight," he growled in my ear. His hands gripped my hips as he plunged out and then back in.

"Yes," I hissed, fighting the restraints. My core clenched tight, picking up his slow rhythm. "Faster. Please." Screw Mason and his no sex rule. If Ty didn't fuck me right now, I was going to internally combust.

He quickened his pace, his downward strokes scraping against that exact spot in my body that made me scream.

Fire consumed me. Unable to stand it, I tossed my head back and forth.

His chest heaved against my back. He thrust faster and faster.

My vision flickered. I made noises I didn't even recognize. "More. Oh, God. More."

He gave me everything I craved.

Tied down and spread out on my belly, I was helpless to do anything but succumb to him and the soul-shattering orgasm that exploded inside me.

As I clamped down on him, he came with a shout and blasted me with a hot rush of liquid heat.

For the first time in hours, the raging fire went away. Feeling sated and happy, I sagged against the bench.

"Thank you," he said, his large body blanketing my back.

"No, thank you," I panted. "You're mine."

"I'm yours," he said, laying a feather light kiss on my back.

As the soul bond snapped between us, his joy and love flooded me carrying with it all his memories of us.

Tears filled my eyes. "I've missed you, Sugar Bear."

❄ 17 ❄

MASON

The walls of the dilapidated cabin seemed to be closing in on me. The frustration of not being able to help my mate or my friends was driving me out of my mind. It didn't help that the lingering scent of Havana's sensual musk hung in the air.

This might be the last time I'll smell her. I kicked that thought away before it could drag me into a deep depression.

I rocked faster in the rocking chair, finding the motion soothing. When I felt calm enough to speak, I pressed the talk button on the radio in my hand. "How's it going at the resort, mates?"

No one responded for a full minute. Finally, Gabriel's voice came on. "We're taking out as many reanimated as we can from the window. They've surrounded the hotel, but the humans have done a good job barricading themselves inside."

"How many are left?"

"At least two hundred."

Bloody hell. They and the humans were in grave peril. "Let me help. If I left now, I could be there within an hour." Now that I could take hybrid form, I could eliminate the reanimated with no risk of harm to myself. Other than the loss of my reason and logic, that is. The one time I'd taken that form, a haze had come over my mind and I'd been ready to tear apart Havana's other mates. I didn't welcome the thought of returning to that feral state, but if it would save everyone, I'd do it in a heartbeat.

"We've got this," Gabriel said with way too much arrogance for male facing certain death. "But we have some bad news."

As if Havana's capture and a zombie invasion isn't enough. I sighed. "What is it?"

"You know that annoying human male."

"Marshall," Liam called out.

"Yeah, that guy. He injected himself with the last syringe of Havana's blood."

Shocked, I stopped rocking. "What happened?"

"Well, let's just say, we don't have to listen to him running his mouth any more."

My stomach dropped. "Havana's blood killed him?"

"Death by Lykos blood poisoning," Gabriel confirmed.

Christ. I'd thought for sure Havana's blood would be the Z-virus cure for both humans and latent Lykos, but it appeared it was only effective on our kind. Although that was a boon for young Lykos who hadn't yet transitioned, it wasn't the savior for humanity I was hoping it might be.

I drummed my fingers on the rocking chair armrest. Perhaps cellular modifications to Havana's blood would allow humans to tolerate—

Nathan's voice interrupted my thoughts. "Mason, I've just heard from Ty. He's inside Sanctuary and he's getting Havana out through an underground tunnel. I'll need you to meet them and bring them somewhere safe. Ty doesn't sound like he's at full strength and we don't know what condition Havana is in."

Relief and excitement shot through me. *This is the opportunity we've been hoping for.* "Where is the tunnel?"

As soon as Nathan gave me the location, I bolted out the door. Following his directions, I hiked through the snow to a small cave-like opening in the base of a mountain a couple miles away. The opening was only three feet in diameter, but Havana shouldn't have any problem crawling out of it. I didn't see or scent her anywhere. *Where are they?*

"I'm in position, but I don't see them," I said into the radio.

"There's been a complication. The access to the tunnel has been walled off on their end. Can you try to break through it?"

"You want me to go inside?" I'd been claustrophobic all my life and no part of me wanted to be crawling through miles of underground tunnels in the dark. "Is there another way to get them out?" *Any other way.*

"No. Go through the tunnel."

I eyed the tunnel opening with no amount of eagerness. "Perhaps I could infiltrate Sanctuary from the east side. There are only four Enforcers guarding that portion of the compound. I could take my hybrid form and—"

"For fate's sake climb your ass in there, Mason. Havana needs you."

She needs me. My chest swelled with purpose. There wasn't anything I wouldn't do for my mate. Sucking in a deep breath, I got on my hands and knees and crawled through the hole. The musty smell of decay and frozen earth choked me as I ducked past gnarled roots and inched over jagged rocks.

Nearly twenty meters in, the passage narrowed. The fit was tight and I struggled to push my newly expanded body through. At one point, I was forced to army crawl on my stomach for nearly a mile. Then, I got stuck between two large rocks.

Some bloody hero I am. I couldn't even reach the radio to call for help, not that the others were in any position to assist me.

I'm trapped.

Immediately, my old boyhood fears locked my muscles in place. The earth seemed to tighten around me, preparing to swallow me whole.

Bloody hell. I'll die down here. I'd never find the cure for the Z-virus. I'd never discover the truth about my biological family. And I'd never get a chance to tell Havana goodbye.

That last one hurt more than all the others. Havana's beautiful face appeared in my mind.

I'm so sorry, my love.

All at once I sensed her. *She's close!* Our mental channel was still dark, but just knowing she was in proximity filled me with renewed determination. *I have to save her.* I shoved myself through, not caring that one of the jagged rocks lacerated my side. Ignoring the bleeding, I crawled for another mile and then blessedly the tunnel opened up to the point I could stand. Three meters away there was a junction.

The main passage continued, but above my head was a large opening in the top of the tunnel. Dangling from inside the opening was a frayed rope as thick as my wrist.

I sensed the rope would bring me to my mate, but I needed to be sure. I radioed Nathan. "Hey, mate. I've come to a rope —"

"Climb the rope," he said in a strained voice. "That will take you to the area just outside the playroom."

"The what?"

I could hear deafening explosions in the background.

"Just climb the rope," Nathan said before ending the transmission.

I grabbed the rope and climbed the not insignificant distance upward. At the top was a cavernous space littered with masonry materials and debris. The back of the space dead-ended into a brick wall.

The overwhelming sense that Havana was close drew me toward the wall. I rested my hands against the bricks. My mate was just on the other side. I'd bet my soul on it. *But how to get through?*

I picked up a dusty triangular-shaped trowel and tried stabbing the wall with the pointed end. When that didn't work, I tried hammering the wall with the large wooden end of the trowel. It snapped off. *Bollocks.*

I gritted my teeth in frustration, but stopped short of radioing Nathan again. The Alpha had his hands full and it was obvious what I'd need to do next. After checking that the ceiling was a safe distance up, I stepped out of my loafers, shucked my clothes, and focused on transforming into the hybrid.

After a moment, my muscles and tendons lengthened and my bones and cartilage snapped. Once I'd assumed the beastly shape, a haze fell over me as if my mind were being hijacked by something primitive and feral. A rumbling growl shook my chest. I needed my mate and that wall was in the way.

I stomped over to the bricks and slammed my fist through them. They crumbled like Styrofoam. I tore the wall down angered to find yet another barrier in the way. It looked like the back of a bed. I shoved it hard. The bed flew across the floor, landing a meter from the dark-skinned male who was screwing a restrained female.

The male let out a shout of surprise and I glimpsed the ebony hair of the female hogged-tied down underneath him.

Havana.

This fucker was raping my mate. Rage like nothing I'd ever felt in my life gripped me. I barreled through the hole in the wall and charged the male who dared hurt her.

"Mason?" Havana cried.

The male withdrew from my mate and raised his hands in front of him. The male appeared underfed and weak. *He's no match for me.*

Havana fought her restraints. "Mason, stop!"

I'd free her once I'd dealt with her abuser. I grabbed the male by the throat and flung him into the bars of a metal prison. His body made a satisfying crunch, but it wasn't enough. He needed to pay.

As I stalked over to him, he struggled to stand. Blood trickled from the corner of his mouth and one of his legs gave out. "W-who are you? What are you?" His scent of fear and confusion only fueled my anger.

I bared my teeth in a show of aggressive dominance. *"I'm the last face you'll see before you die!"*

"Stop now!" the male shouted, infusing his voice with power.

His attempts at compulsion only further enraged me. I raised my fist over his head.

"Mason, don't hurt him! He's my mate!" Havana screamed.

Her words permeated my frenzied mind. I realized this was Tasha's Alpha male son, Tyberius. *Nathan said he's helping Havana escape.* I looked back at my mate.

Havana's eyes were frantic and she yanked against the restraints. Forgetting about the male, I stomped over to her and shredded the straps binding her to the leather bench with my claws. Then I snapped the silver band wrapped around her head.

Immediately she sat up and flung her arms around my waist. "Mason! Thank God." Her relief and happiness poured into me as our mental connection came back online.

I sank into my human form and dragged her against my chest. *"Are you okay, love?"*

She nodded. A spasm wracked her body and she let out a soft moan.

I pulled away to look at her? "Are you injured?"

"She's in heat," Tyberius gasped, before throwing back his head and changing into a dark wolf.

"That's impossible." And yet, the musky scent of her pheromones fogged my brain making me want to lay her back on that bloody bench and take her again and again.

Havana licked her lips. "It's true. It's why I've been so frisky lately."

How can she ovulate in her condition? "But you're—"

Havana interrupted me. "Tasha said it happens sometimes and twins are the result."

I'd never heard of hyper ovulation occurring among Lykos, but then again reproduction wasn't my specialty.

She squeezed my hand as Tyberius shifted back into human form and walked over. "Mason, this is Tyberius, my newest mate."

Tyberius leaned against the black bondage bench or whatever the bloody hell it was and gave me an appraising look. "How does an Original Alpha male escape my mother's notice?"

"Because I'm not an Original," I said, feeling defensive.

"Did you inject yourself with my blood?" Havana glanced at Tyberius. "It seems to turn everyone into an Alpha."

"Gabriel injected me," I said with a frown. I owed the bastard a good ass kicking for forcing such a life altering decision on me.

"Are he and the others coming too?" Havana said, looking back at the hole in the wall.

"No, they're still in the clinic."

"That's why I can't reach them," she said in a breathless voice. She rubbed herself against my thigh.

Her pheromones fogged my brain, making it hard to focus. "We need to go."

Havana shook her head. "I'm not leaving without the children."

"What bloody children?" I asked before remembering in the human children Tina had been so concerned about.

"Isaac and Lily are in danger as long as they're here. I think they are being held downstairs."

Tyberius gave me a look that said he was as frustrated as I was over Havana's stubbornness.

"We can come back for them later, love. The three of us can't take on Tasha and her Enforcers."

"There won't be a later for them if we leave them at Tasha's mercy." She let out a panting breath. "Gabriel, Liam, and Nathan have to come here and help us rescue them."

"That won't be possible. Apparently, you compelled them to stay at the clinic." I decided not to tell her they were under attack. No need to stress her further.

Havana gasped. "Oh, no! I never meant to trap them there. How can I set them free?"

"They'd have to hear your voice," Tyberius answered. "The only way to release them is to go to them."

"Maybe there's another way." I rushed back into the tunnel, retrieved the radio, and pressed the talk button as I walked it back to her. "Nathan, I'm here with Havana and Tyberius."

Nathan cursed. "Why in the fates haven't you left Sanctuary?"

How did he know we hadn't left?

"Is Havana okay?" Gabriel demanded.

"Tell her I love her," Liam shouted.

I motioned at Havana.

She took a deep breath and closed her eyes as if concentrating hard. "You're all free to go. Nathan you can talk to me if you want."

There was a collective pause and then Nathan said, "Liam, run down the hall."

A moment later, Liam let out an audible war whoop.

Nathan came back on the radio. "Thank you, my little wolf. We're free."

Havana squeezed the radio hard enough to crush the plastic. "Nathan, I'm sorry for—" She broke off in a coughing fit.

Tyberius joined her. In between hacking coughs he pointed at the vents in the side of the wall. "Gas... we have to...get... out." His eyes rolled up and he hit the ground face first.

"Ty!" Havana took a wobbly step toward the male and promptly passed out.

Bloody hell. Shaking my head to fight off the sedating effects of the invisible fumes, I took hybrid form. My mind instantly cleared.

"What's happening?" Nathan shouted from the radio.

There was no time to update him. *We have to get to the tunnel.* I slung Tyberius over my back, scooped up Havana, and ran for the hole in the wall.

"Stop right there!"

The power of the command vibrated inside my head and locked my muscles in place. *Fuck! The tunnel is right there.* I tried with every fiber of my being to move forward to no avail.

There was a loud whooshing sound followed by the sound of high heels clicking on the marble floor behind me.

"Somebody update me right now!" Nathan screamed.

Fuck. I looked down at Havana's limp body in my arms. I'd failed her. I pressed her against my fur-covered chest, vowing to do whatever was in my power to save her.

But I wasn't the one with the power right now.

Tasha approached us looking like a goddess with her long blonde hair, burnish gold skin, and citrine eyes.

I shuddered, knowing all too well her stunning beauty disguised a monstrous soul. *"Let us go!"*

Tasha threw back her head and laughed. "And to think, you were the one I threw out." She glanced at the tall gray-haired Enforcer striding over to us. "Look, Zayn. Our son isn't a total disappointment after all."

18

HAVANA

I woke on the marble floor of the playroom with a throbbing pain in the inside of my arm. Disoriented, I briefly wondered why I was staring through prison bars. Then it all came back to me.

Tasha!

Heart pounding, I surveyed the room. Except for Mason, Tyberius, and me, it was empty.

Both Mason and Tyberius were lying nude, side-by-side on the floor with their hands shackled to the bars.

Although my wrists and forehead were banded in silver again, at least I could move freely. A wave of dizziness hit me as I tried to stand. Deciding to crawl instead, I inched over to Ty.

His eyes were closed, but at least he was breathing. *Thank God.*

"Ty," I whispered.

He didn't respond, but Mason lifted his head and looked over at me. "He's still unconscious. Given his quickening pulse, he should wake soon."

"Mason!" I moved around Ty and wrapped my arms

around my golden-haired mate. "What happened?"

He clenched his jaw. "Tasha happened. Or should I say my mother happened."

I sat back in shock. "Tasha is your mother?"

"It seems so." He gave me a grim smile. "All my life I dreamed that my biological parents would be kinder and more loving than my adoptive parents." He rattled his shackles. "Little did I know, I was the product of monsters."

Hating the pain in his voice, I rested my hand on his chest. "I'm so sorry, hon." I inspected his restraints, looking for any weakness. There was none.

Mason scoffed. "And you know the worst part? Tasha confessed that when she realized I was an Omega she told her servant to use me as kindling. I'm only alive because someone named Agnes brought me to the humans instead."

Ty opened his eyes. "Believe me, you were the lucky one. There have been countless times when I wished to trade places with my supposedly dead twin brother."

"We're twins?" Mason asked, studying Ty's face.

For the first time, I noticed similarities in their bone structures and the set of their eyes. Those stunning features had come straight from their gorgeous, psychotic mother.

Ty smiled, his white teeth flashing against his dark skin. "As improbable as it sounds, yes. Mother has long told the story of how she negotiated a mating with Sebastian, one of the Original males to conceive me. She was caught by surprise when she went into heat a second time on the way back to Winterhaven. She was forced to mate with her Enforcers."

Mason nodded. "She said Zayn is my father."

"Is that so?" Ty chuckled. "Small world. Zayn is Nathan's Uncle."

I gasped. "So you and Mason are brothers, and Mason and Nathan are what? Cousins?"

Ty made a noise of agreement.

"So what does that make Mira to him?" I asked Ty.

"She's both his sister and his first cousin once removed," he said without blinking.

"Wow." Mason closed his eyes and let his head drop to the floor.

"Are you okay, hon?"

Mason opened his golden Alpha eyes and for a moment, I mourned that I'd never see his flawless ocean blue gaze again. "It's just that I've been searching for my biological family for decades. To find so many family members in a short while, is overwhelming."

"Most of us aren't homicidal killers," Ty said, showing dimples that made my insides warm. "It's good to meet you, brother." His smile faded as he stared at Mason. "Mother said after our birth, we held each other so tightly, she had to pry us apart. Then later, when I was a child, I made up an imaginary twin brother I'd talk to. Mother grew so concerned she brought Nathan to play with me."

"Nathan!" I exclaimed, scanning the playroom. "Where's the radio?" We had to let him and the others know what happened to us.

"Tasha took it," Mason said in a pained voice. "After she ordered me to tell Nathan, Gabriel, and Liam to come here."

Ty tried to sit up. "You didn't."

Mason bowed his head. "I couldn't fight her compulsion."

Fear for the others gripped me. "They wouldn't come here. They had to know it was a trap."

"Tasha compelled me to tell them you were injured and near death. I told them I couldn't risk moving you and if they came to your side, they could anchor you to life."

"That's a bunch of bullshit. No way Nathan would buy that," Ty said, tension leaving his body.

I didn't share his optimism. As I tried to rub away the blooming bruise on the inside of my elbow, I remembered how I'd saved Nathan from certain death by claiming him and ordering him to stay with me. Perhaps the others thought they could do the same for me.

"They said they were on their way." Mason followed my actions with his gaze. "Is your arm hurting?"

"A little," I admitted. Tasha's Enforcers must've been rough when they moved me to the prison cell.

"Show me?"

When I lifted my arm to show him the large dark bruise, he cursed. "Those arseholes butchered your veins. You'll be lucky if they didn't nick a nerve with their needle."

I clutched my arm to my chest. "They took my blood?"

"And too much of it, based on your pallor." Mason let out a heavy sigh. "Tasha demanded I tell her why her blood was killing all the latents instead of turning them into Alphas like you. I had to explain it was because she was no longer pregnant—"

"But I am," I said, folding my arms around myself. I didn't know what was worse, being used as a broodmare or a blood bank.

Ty made a sound of surprise. "You're pregnant?"

I gave him an apologetic look. "Yeah, I probably should have told you before I claimed you. I come with some baggage."

He smiled. "I am honored to be your mate and help father your young."

Relieved, I leaned down and gave him a kiss. Then I looked over at Mason. "So Tasha took my blood to make Alphas?"

Mason nodded. "I'm so sorry, love."

"It's not your fault."

Mason's eyes filled with regret. "I should have been better prepared for her compulsion—"

Ty interrupted him. "There is no preparing for Mother.

She is like a deadly hurricane that blows in and destroys everything in her path."

"Please don't beat yourself up. I appreciate you trying to rescue me." I leaned over intending to kiss Mason's cheek.

He turned, and my lips touched his.

My skin sparked at the contact and the heat between my legs flared. I kissed him again and when he opened his mouth to say something, I deepened the kiss. He tasted so good.

He gasped as I ran my hands down the length of his smooth tanned chest. I loved all of his new muscles.

Needing to be closer, I straddled him and rocked against him. *That feels so good.*

Mason's cock stiffened.

"How are you able to do this—" I stroked my hand down his hard shaft "—while wearing silver?" The silver cuffs Nathan had worn made him impotent.

Mason shuddered under my touch. "Tasha gave both Ty and I some kind of male potency drug."

"Because this is what she wants," Ty said, his gaze on the two of us.

"What does she want?" I said, trying to follow along. I increased the rhythm of my strokes as burning lust sizzled through me.

Mason groaned and thrust against my hands.

"She wants us to impregnate you."

Ty's words splashed over me like freezing water. I snatched my hand away from Mason's erection, jumped off him, and moved to the other side of the cell.

Immediately, a spasm wracked my body. "Oh, God." My core clenched tight with need. I held my hands to my mouth to muffle my scream. *Why does it hurt so bad?*

"Let me ease your suffering, love," Mason called out.

Unable to resist the need to mate, I crawled over to Mason, pulled up the shirt I was wearing, and positioned myself over his engorged cock. "Are you sure?" I managed to say, my voice raspy. "You said we shouldn't have sex."

"That was before we knew you were in heat." Mason arched off the floor, his crown teasing my entrance.

Needing no more encouragement, I slid down his shaft, one incredible inch at a time. When I was fully seated, I let out a blissful sound, and then I rode him. I took him as hard and fast as I could, grinding down on his length, trying to chase the ache away.

He surged underneath me, his eyes brimming with passion. "Ah fuck, you feel so hot, love."

He wasn't kidding. I felt as if I were burning up. I rolled my hips taking him deeper. Pleasure knotted inside me.

"So close. I'm so close," Mason gasped.

"Give her what she needs," Ty said, his smoldering eyes on the two of us.

The scent of my newest mate's arousal kicked my excitement even higher.

I slammed down on Mason, faster and faster.

His chains rattled as he cried out my name. Then he was coming, filling me with his heat.

"Oh, God," I cried, as my climax hit. Pleasure hurled me straight into an ocean of bliss. Shuddering with the aftershocks, I collapsed over Mason.

"Did that help?" he panted.

I started to say yes, but the relentless need rolled over me again. "More, I need more." I rocked over him, but his cock had softened.

Ty lifted his head. "I've got what you need, Starfire." His golden eyes blazed with desire.

I looked over at his throbbing dick. It was long, hard, and everything I needed. I gave Mason an apologetic look. "Hon, is it okay if—"

"Of course," he said with a smile that squeezed my heart.

Nearly mindless with frenzied need, I dismounted Mason, straddled Ty, and took his shaft deep inside.

"Ah, fuck, you feel amazing." Ty rocked underneath me. His cock was thicker than Mason's and it hit all the right places.

"Yes!" I tightened my thighs around his hips and rode him even harder than I'd ridden Mason. "So good..." I leaned down, brushing my lips against his sweat dampened chest.

He strained against his restraints. "I want to suck on you."

I raised my shirt and leaned forward so he could clamp his lips over my nipple. The wet, heat of his mouth on my sensitive peak was almost too much to bear. I quickened my pace, racing us both to the finish line.

Ty's cock seemed to swell inside me, and then he exploded, bathing me with the heat of his release.

His climax triggered mine. Throwing back my head, I came so hard, my shouts of ecstasy echoed throughout the room. Collapsing down on his chest, I wrapped my arms around him.

"In the embrace where madness melts in bliss, and in the convulsive rapture of a kiss—thus doth love speak," he panted against my hair.

"I love your pretty words, Sugar Bear." I rested my head against his chest, thinking of all the memories he'd shared with me. Once we escaped the nightmare of his mother, we were going stargazing and poetry reading.

I'd hoped the raging fire inside me would ease, but five minutes later the burn was back. Thankfully, Mason was ready for action again.

For the next several hours, I went back and forth mating the brothers until I wore them completely out. Only then did the grinding need finally leave me.

As bone deep exhaustion settled in, I curled up between the brothers and closed my eyes.

"Damn the fates, what have you been doing in here?" a deep voice said near my ear.

"Nathan!" I lifted my head to see the silver-haired Alpha male crouched next to our prison.

Needing to be sure I wasn't just imagining him, I reached through the bars and touched his arm. "Why are you here?"

He pulled my hand to his lips and kissed it. "To rescue you."

"After how I treated you?" He should hate me after unclaiming him and trapping him at the resort.

"I deserve your anger. It would take an entire lifetime to atone for how I've treated you."

I rubbed his soft warm lips. "You've walked right into Tasha's trap."

"I know," he said in a too calm voice.

Ty opened his eyes and lifted his head. "Good to see you, brother."

"Nathan, you shouldn't be here," Mason said, trying unsuccessfully to sit up.

"Clearly," Nathan said, gently prying my hand from his.

"What's your plan?" Ty asked.

Nathan stood and walked the length of our prison. "Release the three of you, and then take care of Tasha once and for all."

That was much easier said than done. I looked up at the ceiling. I didn't see any cameras positioned between the hanging cages, but she had to be monitoring the room somehow. "She gassed us earlier. She could do it again." Then Nathan would be trapped too.

"Don't worry. Liam and Gabriel are keeping Tasha and her Enforcers plenty busy. They even brought some reanimated friends along to play."

I sucked in a breath. "They led zombies to Sanctuary?"

Nathan confirmed with a nod. "And Liam was kind enough to open the front gates."

"There are children here," I said, thinking of Isaac and Lily. I hoped with all my heart they were still alive and in one piece.

Nathan waved his hand dismissively. "The Enforcers will make short work of the dead, but Gabriel and Liam won't be so easy to defeat." He inspected the keyhole on the cage door. "All we need is something long and pointed to pop this lock."

"You can use my hairloom, Daddy," a tiny voice said from across the room.

"Mira!" Nathan exclaimed.

My heart fell through the floor when I saw the child running over, her diamond hairpin in her hand. "Nathan, what are you thinking bringing her here?"

"I didn't." Nathan's eyes glowed with anger and fear as he gazed down at his daughter. "I told you to stay at the lodge."

Mira didn't flinch from his glare. "I wanted to be with you —" she looked over at me "—and Vana. Hi, Vana."

"Bug, go back the way you came. It's not safe for you here." *Oh, God. If Tasha gets her hands on Mira...*

Ignoring me, she walked over to Ty. "Hi, Uncle Ty. Where are your clothes?"

"Damn the fates! Mira you need to leave." Nathan dragged Mira toward the back of the room.

There was a loud grinding noise.

"Watch out!" Ty yelled.

Nathan pushed Mira out of the way as several cages dropped from the ceiling in a thunderous crescendo.

"No!" I shouted when I realized Nathan had been trapped in one.

"Daddy!" Mira ran over to Nathan's cage and rattled the bars.

"It's okay, sunshine," Nathan said, sounding very much not okay. "We still have Plan B."

"I trust you're not talking about these two here," Tasha said, sweeping into the room in a gold, sequined ball gown.

Behind her long serpentine train were several of her Enforcers dragging Liam and Gabriel. Both my mates had been beaten nearly unrecognizable and both wore thick silver collars around their necks.

"Oh, no!" Their bodies looked so broken, it was a wonder they still drew breath. "What did you do to them?"

Tasha feigned a look of surprise. "I didn't lay a finger on them. But they were no match for my new army."

The stomping sound of boots filled the air as dozens of huge, muscular males, dressed head to toe in black leather, marched single-file into the room. Every one of the males stood over six-foot-five, possessed the hugely sculpted muscles of a bodybuilder, and stared at us with Alpha yellow eyes.

Tasha clapped her hands and the Alpha males came to a stop. "Aren't my Enforcers incredible?"

And frightening as hell. Every Enforcer held some kind of instrument of death. I ran my eyes over them cataloging all the guns, knives, swords, and maces.

"Mother, what have you done?" Ty shouted.

"I've made Winterhaven the strongest and most powerful faction in the world," she said with a feral grin. "We only had enough of the whore's blood to ascend forty of my Enforcers, but in time we will ascend them all." Her heels clicked on the marble as she walked over to our prison. "I promise not to bleed you dry."

I spat at her. "Screw you!"

Moving faster than a striking rattlesnake, she reached her hands through and grabbed a fistful of my hair. Then she rammed my skull against the bars so hard my vision blurred and my mouth filled with blood.

"Don't hurt, Vana!" Mira yelled. Jabbing the pointed end of her hairpin in front of her, the little girl attacked Tasha.

Tasha spun around and kicked the little girl into the side of our prison.

"No!" shouted Nathan and Ty.

"Mira!" I scrambled over to where she lay, crumpled like a wilted flower. Before I could reach her, Tasha picked Mira up by the neck. "It's time this abomination joins her sisters in death."

☙ 19 ❧

NATHAN

Seeing my daughter in the hands of her mother was my worst nightmare come to life.

For the last four years, every action and decision I'd made was to prevent this very moment from happening. Keeping a tight rein on the helpless rage and fear exploding inside me, I said, "Don't hurt her, Tasha."

Tasha's gaze flickered to me. "You think to give me orders, Consort?" Her even tone betrayed her mood. She was fucking amused by the situation.

I curled my hands into fists and took a ragged breath, trying to think a way through this. "She's our child."

"Our child is dead," Tasha shouted. Her eyes glistened as she stared at Mira's limp body. "If only I could trade this mistake for our son."

What in the fates is she talking about? Mira was the product of the one and only time Tasha conceived my child. *Is she hallucinating things now?*

Gabriel had been right when he said Tasha had gone completely insane, not that she'd been mentally stable to begin with. We would need more than my bargaining skills to deal with her.

I glanced over at the bloody males on the floor. With Ty, Mason, Havana and me imprisoned, we needed Gabriel and Liam's strength right now.

As if feeling my gaze, Gabriel opened his eyes. He croaked something that sounded like, "Play dead."

I didn't know what he was talking about. I tried to reach him telepathically, but couldn't. Deciding he must not be able to mind speak with his silver collar, I willed the former Head Enforcer to stay down and wait for the right moment to attack.

Turning my attention back to Tasha, I said, "I will give you all the sons you desire. Just don't hurt, Mira." At that moment, I would have promised her anything and everything to save the life of my daughter. She and Havana were the only females I loved, and both were now at the mercy of the Beast. I had only myself to blame. I was the idiot who'd brought them here. I'd all but handed them over to this soulless creature that had tortured and abused me my entire life.

Tasha's eyes glinted for a moment as she looked from Mira to me.

I held back the shudder as I imagined what being with her again entail. Every inch of this fucking playroom, and the ones like it at all Tasha's estates, was filled with my degradation and pain. Memories of the beatings, the stabbings, and the rapes blazed through my mind. I steeled my spine knowing I'd volunteer to go through it a thousand times to save Mira and Vana.

I dared to glance at the female I loved more than life itself. Tremors wracked Vana's body as she pleaded with Tasha to put Mira down. I wanted so badly to apologize for how I treated her. She deserved so much better than me.

Tasha stalked over, carrying Mira like a broken doll.

"You already gave me a son, Nathan. He would have been born in the next few weeks if that bastard Emmanuel Moreau hadn't attempted to assassinate me at the Interfaction Games."

I blinked remembering Gabriel saying Tasha had been pregnant recently. "You're mistaken. I can't have fathered your child."

Tasha let out a cold laugh. "You thought you were so clever, doping yourself on wolfsbane when I was in heat. Stupid male, not all of your body was unconscious that night."

Shock forced me motionless. I had no idea she could manage such a feat, but then again, I should have known she'd gotten what she came for. It explained why I'd woken two days later naked with my fake silver cuffs broken in half next to me on my bedroom floor—no sign of Tasha or her Enforcers in my home. *Fuck.* Willingly or not, I'd impregnated Tasha. Guilt stabbed into me as I saw the look of surprise on Vana's face. Once again, I'd betrayed my mate.

No. She's no longer my mate. Vana had rightfully unclaimed me.

"I didn't know," I whispered to Vana. Then I curled my hands into fists and stared directly into Tasha's eyes. "I can give you another son."

"Tempting." Tasha glanced at the Enforcers lining the wall. "However, I no longer need a son. Not with all these Alpha male warriors at my command."

She stared at the golden-eyed males with pride and excitement. "You will be my sons now. What say you?"

"We serve you, my Alpha!" Their war cries reverberated off the walls and high ceiling.

She turned to me. "See, I don't need you." Looking down at Mira, she said, "And I certainly don't need another faithless, backstabbing, daughter."

Fuck the fates. Think. Think. What else can I bargain with? Her oath was the only thing that came to mind. "You swore you would not harm Mira in return for my council seat."

Tasha gaze narrowed. "I will eliminate the Lykos council."

My mouth fell open. The Lykos high council was treated as sacrosanct by all the factions, to even think of harming them was unfathomable. "You can't mean to—"

She snarled. "Those pretentious assholes refused my petition to extradite Emmanuel for the crime of killing my unborn. I'll kill every last one of them."

"Stop, Mother. You're speaking treason," Ty shouted from his cage.

"Fuck them all," Tasha snarled. "I didn't need their permission to take Emmanuel and punish him for his crimes. By the way, he shared such interesting stories about you, Nathan, and his Aunt Shoshanna during his torture."

Ty paled, realizing as I did, that Emmanuel must've known about our planned coup. *He's the reason Tasha knows of our betrayal. Fuck.* The fates only knew what diabolical punishment Tasha inflicted on Shoshanna in retribution.

"The other faction leaders won't stand for it," Ty called out.

"We will kill them when they arrive too. There will only be one faction, and one ruler over all Lykos." Tasha bared her teeth. "No one will challenge me and my army."

Ty shared my look of horror. His mother was planning to destroy our species' government and entire way of life.

"But first, I need to take out the trash," Tasha lifted Mira.

"No!" I shouted. I knew what I had to do to save those I loved. "If you spare her, I will accept your claim." My soul was the last thing I had left to barter with. Tasha had tried to claim me on more than one occasion. I'd always rejected it until now. "Claim me."

Vana let out a sob, "Nathan, no."

Not daring to take my eyes off the monster holding my

child, I whispered to Vana, "This is the only way." As soon as Tasha claimed me, I'd kill myself. Since our souls would be bound, she'd die with me.

"No!" Vana pleaded.

Tasha would sense any physical attack on her, but she couldn't foresee me harming myself. A world without the Beast was the last gift I could give Mira and Vana.

Tasha went motionless. "You'd accept my claim?"

"Yes." I was already scanning the room for the best weapon to take my life.

Tasha smiled even wider. "What perfect irony that you are finally ready to give yourself to me, but I have forty other Alphas to choose from." She walked over to a dark-skinned enforcer and ran her hands down his chest.

The poor male didn't move a muscle, but I saw the flare of panic in his eyes.

Tasha patted his stomach and turned her gaze back to me. "Although I admit, no one suffers quite like you Nathan. Seeing your daughter die might actually break you." She choked Mira.

I slammed myself at the bars of my cage trying to get to her. "No!"

Zayn, of all males, stepped forward. "Mistress, stop." I'm sure I only imagined the distressed look in his eyes. He was supposedly my father's brother, but he'd never tried to protect me from the abusive tyrant he slavishly served.

"Yes?" Tasha hissed.

Zayn cleared his throat. "It's bad luck to break an oath."

Tasha rolled her eyes. "Fine. You do it then."

The cursed male bowed and took my daughter from her.

"No. Let me be the one to do it," Gabriel rasped, pushing himself up on his arms.

"You?" Tasha snarled. "The warrior who betrayed me

twice? The only reason you still have your head is because your life is tied to the whore's." She motioned at Vana.

Vana was crouched over Mason. I couldn't see what she was doing. Hopefully, not mating him. Damn the fates, it was a shitty time for her to be in heat.

Gabriel bowed before Tasha. "Please, my Alpha. The whore's beauty seduced me. I know now that I made a mistake. I want to serve you and only you." He stared at the long line of Alpha males. "And I want to lead the strongest fighting force this world has ever seen." There was no faking the covetous look in his eyes.

"Zayn will lead them," Tasha sneered. "You will spend the rest of your days in my dungeon."

Gabriel scoffed. "Zayn is past his prime. You once said I was the greatest Head Enforcer you'd ever had. Let me prove that to you again." Gabriel lifted his arms.

Every Enforcer in the room pointed their weapon at him.

Showing no fear, Gabriel brought his hands to his face and with a sickening squelch gouged out his own eyes.

Havana turned to look at him and screamed.

Fuck the fates. The male didn't even let out a whisper of a sound as he ripped his eyes from their sockets and presented them to Tasha. "Give me one more chance, my Alpha."

When Tasha did not take his offering, Gabriel laid the bloody orbs on the floor in front of her and bowed his head. Blood poured from his empty eye sockets and splashed onto the white floor.

Tasha looked down at Gabriel as if in contemplation. For some unfathomable reason, she'd always had a soft spot for the insufferable jackass. *Will that and his blood sacrifice persuade her to forgive him?*

Tasha nodded as if coming to a decision. Then she slid her long dagger from her thigh sheath and handed it to him. "Slay the child with this."

Gabriel kissed the blade.

I took a deep breath to keep my fear at bay. *The asshole has a plan. He has to have a plan.*

As Zayn set Mira in front of Gabriel, I gripped the bars of my cage. If only I could get free.

I spared a quick look at Vana's prison. Inside it, Mason was getting to his feet, Ty was shaking off his shackles, and Vana was using Mira's hairpiece to remove her silver bands. If they were going to do something they had to hurry.

Every eye was on Gabriel as he leaned down over Mira and muttered something. Then he rose above her with the blade lifted. "I do this for Winterhaven."

"Kill her now, Gabriel!" Tasha shrieked, her voice shaking with power.

Oh, fuck no! There was no way Gabriel could fight Tasha's compulsion.

The warrior's arms trembled.

Hope bled out of me. I shouted my daughter's name wanting my voice to be the last thing she heard.

Gabriel brought the weapon down.

Zayn darted forward as if to grab the blade, but Gabriel suddenly threw it at Tasha.

"You fool!" Tasha ripped the blade out of the air before it could touch her. "You know better than to attack m—" She was interrupted by a tremendous roar that shook the cages still hanging from the ceiling.

Gabriel slid back to allow Mira, who'd taken hybrid form, to stand.

In an impressive show of strength, my daughter roared again and gnashed her dagger-like teeth at Tasha.

Tasha gaped at her for a second. Then, seeming to remember herself, she snarled at Mira. "One little hybrid is no match for me."

"What about me?" yelled Mason, shoving the prison door

open. The lock fell to the floor, my daughter's butterfly hairpin inside. The blond male lifted his shackle-free wrists and took his monstrous hybrid form.

The sight of the doctor's massive jaws, and gleaming gold fur brought a collective gasp from the Enforcers.

"And what about me, Mother?" shouted Ty, stepping out of the same cell. With a toss of his head he assumed an even larger hybrid form.

Shocked beyond words, I stared at the bristling black fur coating Ty's bestial body. In all our years together, I'd never known Ty held the power of the Originals.

Based on Tasha's look of surprise, neither had she. "Y-you have the gift, Tyberius?"

His answering howl sent murmurs of unease rippling through the Enforcers. No doubt seeing three creatures whose strength and near immortality were legend among our species scared them shitless.

Tyberius stomped over to my cage and ripped off the door.

I stepped out, still in awe of his ability. *"Brother, you kept this secret all this time?"*

He lowered his snout, to look at me. *"I feared what you would think of me and I feared Mother using me as a weapon."*

I clapped him on his furry back. "Someone wise once told me that a life lived in fear is no life, brother." Squaring my shoulders, I faced the Alpha of Winterhaven. No longer would Tasha rule us all in fear and blood. "I stand with these others against you."

Tasha's fury-filled gaze bounced between Ty and me. "I raised you both—gave you two everything you could ever want, and you reward me with betrayal?"

"You gave us nothing but pain and suffering," I said, leveling an accusing gaze at Zayn.

The senior Enforcer looked away as if ashamed.

Gabriel rose, turning his empty eye sockets on Tasha. "I stand against you."

Liam jumped to his feet. "I too, stand against you!" He bulldozed through the Enforcers standing around him and punched his giant fist through a nearly invisible panel on the side wall.

The hanging cages fell.

HAVANA

As the metal cages dropped from the ceiling, Tasha and the Enforcers rushed toward the door. *I can't let them escape.* Putting every bit of strength and power into my voice, I shouted. "Freeze."

Everyone, except Zayn, turned into statues.

The gray-haired Enforcer rushed to Tasha's side only to be trapped by the large silver cage that fell over the two of them.

A riot of emotions crashed over the bitch's face—confusion, disbelief, and then helpless rage. "How can you have more power than me? You were just a half-human whore."

"So much better than being a psychotic monster," I clapped back.

Tasha's gaze filled with cold fury. "Attack them!" she yelled to the dozen Enforcers who hadn't been trapped by the cages. But those warriors were frozen too. "Zayn do something!" she shrieked to the Enforcer standing behind her.

Zayn bowed his head at me in respect.

"It's game over for you, bitch," I said, stepping around their cage. "You won't hurt anyone ever again." I put a healthy kick of compulsion in my voice.

Tasha shrieked. "I'll crush every bone in your body then leave you to die—" She stopped mid-sentence as if she could somehow see Zayn lifting his curved sword behind her.

Her eyes went wide. "Stop! Zayn you serve me!"

Seeming unswayed by her attempt at compulsion, Zayn brought down his blade, slicing her head clean off.

Shocked silence descended in the room.

"Now she'll hurt no one," Zayn announced.

Holy shit. I opened and closed my mouth, not knowing how to respond. I watched in fascinated horror as Zayn pulled off his shirt and laid it over Tasha's corpse.

"Beautiful, do you mind unfreezing us?" Liam shouted, bringing my attention back.

Realizing that I'd frozen my mates as well as my enemies. I called out, "All my allies are free."

Immediately, Tyberius, Nathan, Mason, Liam, and Mira broke from their statue poses along with several Enforcers I didn't know.

Liam and a handsome dark-skinned male tried to assist Gabriel whose legs had given out.

"Gabriel!" I cried rushing to his side.

"I did it," he gasped. "I overcame the Beast's compulsion.... If only I could have done it earlier.... For Isla."

He wasn't making any sense. Blood ran like crimson ribbons from the holes where his eyes should have been. *He needs to shift.* I tugged on the huge silver collar around his neck. "We need to take this off."

Mira nudged me, her snout cold against my arm.

I turned to her. "Can you break this?"

In answer, she reached out and wrenched the collar apart. The metal pieces hit the floor with a clank.

Gabriel immediately shifted. His movements were so fast I barely registered his wolf form before he wore his human skin again. "Thank you," he gasped, opening his regenerated eyes to look at Mira.

Mira's tongue lolled out of her mouth, and for a moment she looked more like a dog than a monster.

"Can you help me out?" Liam asked, leaning down so Mira could reach his neck.

Mira snapped his silver collar too.

Liam shifted to his russet-colored wolf and back, letting out a heavy sigh when he'd healed. "Thank you, Mira."

Despite her beastly form, Mira looked somewhat bashful as she ducked her shaggy head into my hair.

My heart squeezed with pride for how strong and courageous she'd been. If not for her and her butterfly hairpin, things could have gone very differently. Hoping what she'd seen today hadn't scarred her for life, I rubbed the tuffs of her ears and coaxed her into her human form.

When she was a little girl once more, she wriggled out of my embrace and ran to her father. "Daddy!"

Nathan scooped her up and planted kisses over her face. "You were amazing, sunshine."

"Very impressive, Miss Mira," added Mason who'd taken his human form along with Ty. The two brothers knotted towels around their waists, a gesture I appreciated.

Ty nodded. "That was pretty spectacular, niece." He grabbed another towel from the shelf and draped it over Mira.

Mira grinned. "Gabe told me to play dead. Then he told me to attack."

I gave the dark-haired male a look of thanks, but Gabriel was too busy working with Liam to release Zayn from the cage he shared with Tasha's corpse.

Once the guys ripped the door off, Zayn took the hand Gabriel offered him and stepped out. "Thank you."

Gabriel shook his head. "I never thought I'd see the day when you turned on your master, Zayn."

"I'm sorry it took so long to break the chains of my servitude." Zayn looked from Gabriel to Mason. "I was conscripted to the Winterhaven Enforcers when I was just a babe... Tasha's rule is all I've ever known." He turned to give Nathan an apologetic look. "I'll never forgive myself for standing by while Tasha abused you. Please know I would never allow any harm to come to Mira."

That slightly increased my estimation of him, but I needed to know if Isaac and Lily had survived. "What about the two human children Tasha imprisoned? Are they okay?"

He nodded. "They are alive and well downstairs."

"Thank God." I let out a huge sigh of relief.

Zayn's gaze shifted to Mason. "It was me who compelled Agnes to bring you to the humans when you were a babe. I hope your family treated you well."

Mason strode over and put his arm around me. "Havana, Mira, and these males are my family." He nodded at Nathan, Ty, Gabriel and Liam.

Nathan stayed where he was, but Ty, Gabriel, and Liam stepped closer.

They are my family too. I felt such overwhelming love and devotion from each of my mates, it brought tears to my eyes.

"Vana's going to be my mommy," Mira called out from Nathan's arms.

"Shh, Mira." Unnamed emotion flashed in Nathan's eyes when he looked at me. "I'm sorry," he mouthed.

My heart twisted and the tatters of our severed bond seemed to throb. *Is there hope for us getting back together?*

Zayn gave me a curious look. "Who are you exactly?"

Nathan stepped forward, coming to stand next to Mason. "Havana James is our Alpha, and the leader of the—" He gave me a quick look. "*What do you want to call your faction?*"

My mind went blank.

Without missing a beat he said smoothly, "—Sanctuary faction."

Sanctuary faction. I liked the sound of that.

"In that case." Zayn fell to his knees before me. "I pledge my life and service to you, Alpha of Sanctuary."

Uncertain how to respond, I looked at Nathan. *"Do I accept?"*

He slowly nodded. *"Zayn is one of the greatest strategists in the territory. However, I would advise compelling him not to betray you just to be safe."*

"No!" I raised my voice. "Know this, in my faction, no compulsion of any kind will be allowed from this moment forward. And I include myself in that."

The Enforcers looked stunned and began speaking in hushed whispers to each other.

Gabriel reached out to touch my arm. "Princess, do not give up your power—"

I held up my hand to stop him. "Only pain can come from stripping others of their will." I knew all too well how it felt to have my mind violated—my choices and memories taken from me.

Nathan and Ty exchanged an uncomfortable look.

Mason tightened his arm around me. *"That's very noble."*

"Thank you." I'd been called a lot of things in my life, but that was a first. Maybe this whole Alpha thing was making me a better person... werewolf... whatever.

Zayn's brows rose as if in surprise, then his lips curled upward. For a moment his resemblance to Mason was so uncanny, I blinked. Then the older male said, "You're not at all like Tasha are you?"

"Hell, no."

"Good. I'm yours to command, my Alpha." Zayn kissed the floor by my foot.

"Okay," I said, not sure if I was supposed to say something more regal sounding.

The handsome dark-skinned warrior knelt before me. "I'm Ambrose. I also pledge myself to you, my Alpha." He pressed his lips to my toes.

I gasped. *Wow.* He was one sexy male.

"I accept," I said, trying to tug the hem of Nathan's shirt down to cover more of my thighs

He moved his lips to the top of my foot, and then grinned up at me. "I'm willing to do anything for my Alpha. Anything..."

"That's enough," Gabriel said, smacking him on the head.

An Enforcer named James shoved Ambrose out of the way and knelt in front of me. He was followed by dozens of others until every male in the room, including the Enforcers in the cages, had sworn themselves to me.

Overwhelmed by the adoration in my new followers' eyes, I whispered to Mason, "Why are they doing this?"

"We have a primal instinct to serve and protect a single adult Alpha female. It's in our DNA. With Tasha gone, these males now want to be part of your faction. They want you to lead them, love."

Crap. That was a lot of responsibility for someone who hadn't even finished high school. As my adrenaline faded, a bone weary exhaustion set in. My knees threatened to give out.

Mason tightened his arm around me, to keep me upright. "You need to rest."

"I can carry her back to our room," Liam said, reaching his arms out.

When I didn't step into them, a worried look crossed his face. "Assuming you don't mind me touching you."

"Of course I don't mind you touching me. I love you, big guy," I reached my hand out, and he took it.

Liam gently folded his fingers around mine. *"I'm sorry for being an ass back at the lodge."*

"Me too," added Gabriel, a solemn look on his face.

I had to tease the male. *"What are you saying exactly, Gabriel?"*

Gabriel strode over and stared down at me. "I'm sorry, princess. I'm sorry for making decisions without consulting you. I'm sorry for being pig-headed and rude. I'm sorry for all the times I upset you in the past and all the times I will probably upset you in the future. Is that a good enough apology?"

"Yes," I said, rising on my toes to kiss him.

His smoke and leather scent surrounded me as he pressed his warm lips to mine.

I moaned, rubbing my body against his.

Gabriel nibbled my lips, and I about lost my mind. If not for Mason clasping my right hand and Liam grabbing my left, I might have pushed Gabriel to the floor and mounted him. Clearly, my heat hadn't completely gone away.

"Perhaps we should go somewhere more private, love?" Mason whispered into my ear.

Becoming aware of the dozens of very interested eyes on me, I nodded.

Mason must've said something privately to the others, because my mates snapped into action.

Liam pushed Ambrose, James, and Zayn out of our way. "Our Alpha is leaving."

Zayn bowed to me. "Please summon me when you wish to discuss your plans for ruling Sanctuary and Winterhaven."

Gabriel gave him a sour look. "What makes you think you'll be involved in the decision making, old-timer?"

Zayn stiffened. "Tasha reinstated me to Head Enforcer when you betrayed her."

Gabriel stepped into the male's face. "I'm in charge and—"

I cleared my throat. "I'm in charge."

Gabriel bowed low. "Of course, my Alpha."

That's more like it. Hiding my smile, I said, "Zayn, please brief Nathan, my Head Mate, and Gabriel, my Head Enforcer, on the current state of Sanctuary and Winterhaven. The two of them will provide me with a recap later."

Nathan's look of surprise and Gabriel's look of frustration were priceless.

Nathan set Mira down. "I need to talk to Vana for a minute, sunshine."

Mira wrapped her towel around her waist trying to copy Ty and Mason. "And I need to find my hairloom."

"I know right where it is, Miss Mira," Mason said, leading her away.

After exchanging an awkward look, Ty and Liam stepped away, giving Nathan and I a moment alone.

"Do you still want me?" Nathan asked, hope brightening his amber eyes.

Of course I wanted him. I was pissed as hell at how Nathan had treated me, but his willingness to risk everything to rescue me along with his readiness to sacrifice himself to the female who'd tormented him his entire life showed his true heart. I still loved him, but I wasn't going to let him off that easily. "It means I may have a position for you."

"*Yeah,*" he intoned. *"And what are the job requirements?"*

"We can discuss them at the Head Mate interview. Your bedroom in an hour. Don't be late."

A slow panty-melting grin spread over his face. *"I won't."* He turned to Zayn and began speaking to the older male in a low voice.

Gabriel cursed. "Working with Nathan will be pure torture."

Or it could bring the two hardheaded males together. I hoped, anyway. "Not if you two work as a team."

Gabriel mumbled something under his breath and stalked over to speak with Nathan and Zayn.

I noticed Ty standing by himself staring at the cage with Tasha's body. Through our bond, I felt his mixed emotions—anger, relief, and sadness.

Even though his mother had treated him horribly, she was still his mother. Fighting back my fatigue, I walked over and put my hand around his waist. "Are you okay, Sugar Bear?"

He gave me a sad smile. "Mother wasn't always a ruthless monster. But her death was long overdue. The world is safer now. We are safer now." He squeezed my shoulder and glanced at Nathan, Gabriel, and Zayn. "Do you mind if I speak to Zayn about releasing the prisoners in Tasha's dungeon?"

"Not at all. See that everyone is freed." God only knew how many poor souls Tasha had imprisoned. "Please make sure the children downstairs are let go right away." I wanted nothing more than to see them, but my head was spinning so badly I had to grit my teeth to stay standing.

After Ty moved away to join the others, I took a step and nearly fell. "I've got you, Beautiful," Liam said, sweeping me into his arms.

I rested my head against his massive chest. "Thank you, big guy."

"I'm not too big for you, am I?" Liam asked, carrying me out of the playroom. His face stayed neutral, but I could feel his anxiety through our bond.

I wrapped my arms around his neck. "Remember, I find tall men incredibly sexy. The bigger, the better." I gave him my sultriest smile.

He grinned. "Really?"

I ran my hand down his stomach. "I can't wait to discover all the upgrades to your equipment." A yawn ruined my attempt at seduction.

He chuckled, striding into our bedroom. "Maybe after some rest." He started to set me down on the bed, but I directed him toward the bathroom.

As much as I wanted to crawl between the sheets and sleep forever, I needed a shower in a bad way. I stank of chlorine and more sex than any person should have in an afternoon.

Liam gently set me down on the tile.

As soon as my toes hit the floor, I tore off Nathan's shirt and darted into the massive shower. A quick crank of the faucet and hot water poured from the elegant rainfall shower-heads mounted on the ceiling. Feeling blissfully relaxed, I grabbed a bar of fragrant soap from a nook in the wall and lathered it.

"I'll be right out here when you need me," Liam said, stepping out of the bathroom.

I closed my eyes, savoring the caress of the water and the fact that I was alone for the first time in hours. Some reflex had me dropping my hands to my belly. *Well, not quite alone.* Was it my imagination, or was my stomach a bit rounder? *How fast did a Lykos baby grow? Or babies...*

Crap. After all the sex I'd had with Mason and Ty, I probably had ten babies inside me. Refusing to dwell on that, I scrubbed my body from head to toe. "Sorry about all this craziness, little one. Life isn't normally so wild."

As I rinsed my hair, I continued talking. "I wish I could promise you things will calm down, but I'm not sure they will." My mind went to all those Alpha male Enforcers. "How the heck am I supposed to lead all those warriors and run a Lykos faction by myself?"

"Not by yourself," Nathan said, opening the shower door. "You'll have me to help you."

❦   21   ❦

HAVANA

I started at the sight of the silver-haired male. "It hasn't been an hour, has it?"

Nathan grinned. "I strive to be early to appointments."

Feigning annoyance, I crossed my arms. "I told you to meet me in the bedroom."

"Liam passed out on the bed. His snores are literally shaking the room."

Trying to bite back my laugh, I peered around his shoulder. "Where's Mira?"

"Mason and Ty took her downstairs to meet the human children. I told Mira not to show the humans her furry face, but since I can't compel her anymore..." He shrugged.

I rolled my eyes. "There's this thing that humans use to manage their children called discipline."

"You try discipling her," he said under his breath.

"Okay." I smiled. Mira could be a handful, but it wasn't anything some positive reinforcement and clear boundaries couldn't address. "Where is Gabriel?"

"On the radio with Tina." He held up his hand as if

expecting my question. "All the humans at the resort, except for Marshall, are fine. We can bring them here tomorrow."

"I would like that."

"What else would you like?"

I licked my lips, feeling my fatigue leave me. "You. In here with me."

Holding my stare, he yanked off the pants he'd been wearing. He was so damn sexy, any delusions I had of resisting his charm evaporated.

While I greedily drank in the sight of his gorgeous bronze skin, he stepped into the shower. "Ah, damn the fates that feels good." He leaned over and grabbed the soap from my hands. "Tell me more about the Head Mate position."

"The what?" My mind blanked as I watch him lather his hair, face, and chest. The soapsuds dripped down the taut abs of his stomach drawing my gaze to his growing erection. As my legs went rubbery, I took a step back and sat on the shower bench.

He reached between his legs and stroked the soap over his swollen cock. "What are the job requirements?"

I pursed my lips knowing I desperately needed to get control back of the situation. "Let's see. The candidate must be smart, have a sense of humor, and be open to new things in and out of the bedroom."

"Check," he said, giving his swollen flesh a few mouth-watering pumps.

Holy crap. Watching him touch himself made my blood sizzle. "The candidate must be good with kids and open to having lots of them." I rubbed my stomach.

"Check." His eyes flared with heat. "Not only do I adore children, I find pregnant females incredibly alluring."

Interesting. "Most important, the candidate must be willing to put up with my other mates with no terms or conditions."

He lowered his gaze to the tile for a moment and then looked back at me. "I will learn to share."

"Good. Finally, the candidate should be good with his hands and mouth." I toyed with my nipples.

He went still, his eyes tracking my every movement. "Can I begin my duties now?"

"In the spirit of negotiation, shouldn't you pledge yourself to me first?" I motioned him to kneel. I'd only been half kidding, but Nathan sank down on his knees in front of the bench.

He bowed low. "I pledge my life and soul to you, my Alpha."

I sat in stunned silence, while the hot water beat down on the two of us. In the entirety of our relationship, Nathan had never taken a subservient role. To have him recognize me as his Alpha was huge. Something big had shifted between us.

When I said nothing after another minute, he looked up at me. "I'm yours if you still want me." The uncertainty in his eyes spurred me into action.

I reached out and cupped his face. "I love you, Nathan. You've always been mine. You'll always be mine."

"I'm yours," he whispered. His eyes shone with emotion as our mating bond fused back into place. The invisible threads binding us together pulsed stronger than ever. "I love you, my little wolf." The intensity of his devotion jolted me.

"You weren't ever going to leave me, were you?"

He shook his head. "How could I live without my chosen?"

"Argh!" I punched his shoulder. "You're a real pain in the ass sometimes, you know that?"

"But you love me anyway, right?" He pulled me forward so he could wrap his arms around my waist.

I leaned over, hugging him. "I do. God help me, I do." I

closed my eyes savoring the emotional closeness we once again shared.

After a moment, he pulled away and nudged my knees apart. Then he kissed the inside of my thigh. "So did I get the job?" The heat sparking in his eyes made me breathless.

"Yes." I slung one leg over his shoulder. "When can you start, Nathan James?"

His reply was muffled, but based on the toe-curling orgasm he gave me, I was pretty sure it was, "Immediately."

Later. Much later, after we'd loved so hard and long that the water ran cold, and we'd collapsed on the floor of the shower, there was a knock at the door.

"We're all waiting. How much longer are you going to be?" Gabriel shouted.

"As long as we want, Enforcer," Nathan shouted back.

"They're all waiting for us?" I mentally sought my mates. Instead of finding them calm and content, they seemed on edge. "Something is going on in there."

When Nathan didn't move, I nipped his shoulder.

"Mmm. That's what I'm talking about." He gave me a slumberous look and shifted his hips.

The brush of his swelling cock against my core made me moan. *How can I possibly want sex again?*

He palmed my breast and laved my nipple with his tongue. "Want to go for round seven?"

As tempting as that was, amazing smells were wafting in from the other room. "I'll have to take a rain check. I'm starving and the guys want to talk to me." About what I didn't have a clue. None of them were responding to my telepathic questions, but at least I'd determined they were excited more than worried.

With a grumble, Nathan stood, turned off the water, and helped me to my feet. Then he made a big show of finding the softest towel and drying me off.

Gabriel knocked again. "If you don't get out here soon, Liam's fucking head will explode."

"We can't have that." I wrapped the towel around me and stepped into the bedroom. The space had been transformed.

The king bed was pushed toward the window making way for a long oak table filled with turkey, mashed potatoes, gravy, fragrant rolls, and even a green bean casserole. There was enough food to feed an army, or at least me and all my mates.

Mason, freshly showered and wearing his signature polo shirt and khaki pants, pulled out one of the wooden chairs set around the table. "I thought you might be hungry."

My stomach rumbled in appreciation of the divine smelling food. "It all looks incredible. How did you have time to cook up a feast?"

Mason flashed me one of his gorgeous smiles. "I can't take all the credit. Agnes had already prepared most of this. However, I did add the casserole, and cranberries." He pointed down at the dishes.

"Aww. Thank you, hon." I took a step toward him when I noticed Liam and Ty positioning a glittering pine tree in the corner of the room.

Both males had showered and dressed too. Ty wore a black long sleeve shirt and pants, while Liam wore a flannel and jeans. As they jostled the tree, snow fell from the lower boughs, along with a string of pearls.

Ty bend down, picked up the pearls, and hung them next to an emerald bracelet.

I let out a gasp when I realized precious gems of every color and size imaginable covered the tree. Mesmerized, I walked over and touched a sapphire and ruby necklace that had to weigh more than my arm.

"Wow." Talk about trimming the tree.

"Do you like it?" Liam asked, pinning a dazzling yellow

diamond brooch to a branch. "I yanked the tree out of the front yard."

Likely with his bare hands. I eyed his Hulk-like muscles appreciatively. "The tree is gorgeous. Where did you get all the bling?"

"Tasha was an avid collector of jewels," Gabriel called out. He crouched down by the fireplace, wearing only a pair of tight jeans. "It's not as if she'll need them anymore." He threw another log into the crackling fire.

Ty held up a popcorn garland. "Should we add this? Mira and the human children made it."

Touched, I smiled. "Then definitely add it. Are they joining us?"

Ty shook his head. "They all went to bed an hour ago. Mira wanted to sleep down in the game room with Isaac and Lily." He looked over at Nathan who stood in the bathroom doorway. "I didn't think you'd mind."

Nathan shrugged. "Today Mira saved us all. She can sleep where she damn well pleases."

"She wanted us to use this as the tree topper," Mason said, pulling the butterfly hairpin out of his pocket and handing it to Liam.

Liam secured the diamond hairpin to the top branch and then put his arm around me. "I wanted to give you a better Christmas than the one you had this morning."

I threw my arms around him. "Thank you. It's perfect."

"Not quite," Nathan said, holding his towel in place as he got down on one knee.

All my mates followed suit and within a heartbeat five gorgeous kneeling males surrounded me. My breathing hitched. "What's going on?"

"Will you marry me?" Nathan held out the gorgeous engagement ring I'd thought I'd lost at the pool.

"Will you marry me?" Mason said, opening a blue velvet

box revealing a dazzling wedding band made up of seven round diamonds.

Liam plucked a breathtaking oval-shaped emerald solitaire ring from the tree and offered it to me. "Will you marry me?"

Gabriel reached into his jean pocket and pulled out a stunning marquise diamond ring. "Will you marry me?"

Ty pulled the gold hoop earring out of his ear and held it out. "Will you marry me?"

Overcome with emotion, I could only spin around looking from one gorgeous male to the next. My eyes watered and I held a hand over my mouth to keep from blubbering.

Liam looked down at his ring and then at me. "These are just placeholders. We wanted you to pick out your rings."

I wanted to tell him how I loved their rings, but I didn't trust myself to speak.

Gabriel shifted to his other knee. "Well? Don't leave us hanging, Princess."

Happiness filled my chest so full, I felt as if I would burst. "Yes. Yes. Yes. Yes. Yes. To all of you!"

My mates rose in unison and took turns kissing me and giving me their engagement rings. Giggling, I inserted Ty's earring into my earlobe and admired my dazzling hand. How I wished I could show my bling to my best friend. Sudden worry for Syd gripped me.

"None of that," Mason chided, always in tune with my feelings. "Tonight is for celebrating."

"Yes. We have so much to celebrate." I rubbed my abdomen.

"And we have so much food to eat," Liam called out, rubbing his own stomach. The big guy tried to sit at the head of the table, but Mason shooed him away.

"Love, come sit here," the doctor said, holding the chair out for me.

As I sat down between Ty and Mason I noticed Gabriel and Nathan still standing.

The two males were exchanging conspiratory looks.

That doesn't bode well. "What's up guys?"

Gabriel grinned. "We were noticing the shackles on the headboard of the bed."

"We think you need to put them on after dinner," Nathan added.

The images that he and Gabriel sent me had me fanning myself. "Wow. When I asked you guys to team up. I didn't quite mean that."

The wicked grins they gave me could've started the bed on fire.

Mason shook his head. "Please postpone your plans to seduce our fiancé until after dinner. I want to make a toast." He held up a bottle of champagne.

Gabriel, Liam, and Nathan quickly sat down.

I peered at the bottle. "Is that Mira's juice?"

"It is," Mason said with a gorgeous smile that heated my blood. "And as your doctor, I give you the okay to have a few sips." He popped open the bottle of champagne and filled each of our glasses. Then he tapped his fork against his glass and stood.

The other males quieted and turned their attention to Mason.

Mason cleared his throat. "I've spent the better part of my life searching for my family. My search brought me across an ocean to a land I'd never heard of and a species I didn't know existed. My search brought me pain—" his expression shadowed for a moment "—and it brought me the most courageous and caring female I've ever met." He reached over and squeezed my hand. "Additionally, it brought me you all, who I proudly call my brothers." He lifted his glass. "To finding our family."

Our mating bonds thrummed with joy and love as we raised our glasses. "To finding our family," we all said in unison.

"I don't know if I ever want this night to end," I said, my eyes brimming with happy tears.

Ty leaned over and kissed my cheek. "Every end is a new beginning, Starfire."

"To new beginnings," the others chanted, raising their glasses again.

Smiling, I dropped my hand to my stomach and whispered, "And happy endings."

Tyberius

The tortured cries of my beloved gutted me. I pressed my hands against the outside of the glass shower door willing the fates to transfer Havana's suffering to me.

The recessed lights over the shower were dimmed, but I had no trouble making out Havana writhing on the ceramic tile floor inside. Her dark wet hair was plastered to her back as she let out another pain-filled cry.

Beside me, Gabriel shifted from one foot to the other. "She should be in the infirmary. It'd be safer to deliver there."

"The children were making too much noise downstairs, remember?" Mira, Lily, Isaac, and the Ackerman children seemed even more excited than we were that Havana had gone into labor. "Besides, Havana wanted to deliver in the shower," I reminded him. And when we tried to talk her out of it, she threatened never to mate with us again.

Our Alpha had been making a lot of threats the past few

hours, but I couldn't fault her for it considering the agony she was in.

Gabriel paced to the bathroom counter and back. "This has gone on too long. Something's wrong."

Liam shoved the dark-haired male. "Stop your doom and gloom, brother. Mason said everything is proceeding perfectly."

Gabriel threw his hands up. "How is this perfect? She's been in there for hours."

Havana's long anguished moan had the three of us turning back to the scene inside the shower.

Nathan sat on the bench behind Havana, bracing her upper body between his legs. "My little wolf, you're doing so well."

"It hurts," Havana cried. "Mason, I changed my mind. I want the pain meds!"

"Sorry, love. You're already dilated to a ten." Seeming not to mind the hot water spraying him in the face, Mason knelt between her legs.

We were beyond fortunate that he'd been here when Havana went into labor. Since generating a human cure for the Z-virus using the blood of the Ackerman children, Mason spent much of his time helping administer the vaccine to as many survivors as he could.

Mason squeezed Havana's knee. "It's time to push, love."

"No!" Havana shook her head from side to side. "Oh, God. It hurts so bad. Why didn't anyone tell me this would hurt so bad?"

"You have to be strong," Nathan crooned into her ear.

"I'd like to see you do this." Havana smacked his face.

I winced in sympathy and rubbed my own black eye. We'd all been taking turns being Havana's support partner, AKA her punching bag. Thank the fates that Nathan, and not I, had ended up with the worst of it.

"Nathan, hold her knees back."

"Ahh!" Havana shrieked.

"That's it. Bear down, love. Just like that. I see the head."

Gabriel, Liam, and I went motionless, our faces pressed against the glass.

Havana screamed loud and long once more.

A moment later the joyous sound of a babe rang out.

"It's a boy!" Nathan announced while Mason snipped the cord. "He's huge!"

"I'd wager close to ten pounds," Mason added.

"He's perfect." Havana let out a half sob, half laugh and took the tiny infant in her arms. "Look at all that red hair, Liam!"

"I see him," the giant said in an awestruck voice. Tears rolled down his face. "I have a son."

"We have a son," Gabriel said, elbowing him in the arm. "He's an Alpha. Did you see those yellow eyes?"

Liam nodded and dabbed his eyes with the hand towel he'd been strangling. "I'll teach him to carve and to hunt. He'll never fear me or hide from me or—"

"Stop blubbering, the babe will love you," Gabriel said, slapping Liam on the back.

"I'd like to name him Gavin after my godson," Havana panted.

We all nodded. It was a fitting tribute for the human boy who'd perished before his time.

"We need to get Gavin's twin out," Mason said, peering between her legs.

The tension in the room ratcheted back up. Thanks to Mason's close monitoring of her pregnancy, we all knew Havana was having twins. However, we hadn't known which of us fathered them.

"Give me one of those deep pushes, love."

Havana let out a low moan and lifted Gavin up to her Head Mate. "Hold him for me."

Nathan took Gavin in his arms and carried him to the shower door.

When I held it open so he could step out, Nathan said, "Tag, you're it."

Fuck!

Liam and Gabriel immediately surrounded Nathan and little Gavin.

Liam sucked in a breath. "He looks just like me!"

"Bring him closer to the vanity light so we can see him better," Gabriel demanded.

I wanted to get a better look too, but Havana shouted, "Where's my support partner?"

Steeling my spine, I stepped into the shower. The hot water blasted my face and clothes as I positioned myself behind her. "I'm here, Starfire."

"Grab her legs," Mason instructed.

As I pulled her knees back, Havana shrieked and panted. "Distract me with some pretty words, Sugar Bear."

Thinking quickly, I recited lines from Havana's favorite poem. "She walks in beauty, like the night of cloudless climes and starry skies—"

Havana let out an ear-splitting cry.

A dark-skinned babe slipped from her body into Mason's steady hands.

Oxygen stalled in my lungs when Mason held him up so we could see his tiny body and thatch of midnight hair. *He's mine!*

Unlike his redheaded twin, this babe quietly regarded us with bright golden eyes.

"He's gorgeous!" cried Havana, bringing him to her chest. "Look at your son, Ty."

Awestruck, I looked down at the tiny male. There were

no poems or words to describe the overwhelming love that rushed through me.

"And I know just what we should name him," Havana said with a weary smile.

"What?" Mason and I asked at the same time.

"Byron."

Laugher rumbled from deep in my chest. *Perfect.* Just like he was. I rested my hand on my son's tiny back. "Welcome to the world, Byron James."

"Let us see him," shouted his other fathers.

Havana, busy delivering the afterbirth, handed him to me.

Gently, ever so gently, I cradled my son into my arms. Then I carried him out into the light where the rest of his family waited to meet him and surround him with their love.

DID YOU ENJOY CLAIMING HER MATES: BOOK THREE?

I'd be so appreciative if you left a review on Amazon or any other reader site or blog you frequent.

If you missed the super sexy bonus shower scene from Claiming Her Mates click here!

⬥

The adventure continues with Sydney's stories.

REFORMING THE WITCH

They imprisoned her. They tormented her. Now they need her to save them...

CLAIMING THE WITCH

A witch... Her warlocks... And some smoking hot shifters...

ABOUT THE AUTHOR

Dia wanted to be a writer from the time she could hold a pencil. A lover of paranormal romance, reverse harem, science fiction, urban fantasy, and horror, she writes action-packed stories featuring kick-butt heroines and the alpha male heroes who fall for them.

If you want to be notified when the next book in the series releases please sign up for my newsletter on my website.

https://diacole.com/

EXCERPT FROM
CLAIMING THE BRIDE

__A night she'll never forget...__

Sophie planned for missing guests and a venue change, but never in her wildest dreams did she foresee the apocalypse happening just days before her wedding. Thankfully, her best men and a dangerous former hitman keep her safe.

Then the unthinkable happens...

Now, Sophie has only hours to live and a decision to make. Will she stay true to her long-lost groom or let her sexy companions give her the wedding night of her dreams?

ore presses his chest into my back. "How about this? We'll do a test, I'm going to touch you here." He cups me between my legs. "If you're wet for me, we do this. If not..." His voice trails off.

I shake my head. That would be so wrong. But the idea has me growing damp and breathless. Even though I'm trapped between his huge body and the desk, I'm filled with excitement not fear.

He waits as if to see if I'll make a move to stop him.

I don't.

He takes my gun and sets it on the desk. Then he slides his hand around my hip, under the waistband of my jeans, and finds the neediest part of my body.

The forbidden touch sends an electric current straight through me.

Tore lets out a shuddering breath. "Ah fuck, you're drenched." His big, callused fingers find my clit.

I can't help moaning loudly. My thighs shake uncontrollably as he strokes me. Pressure builds between my legs. *This feels so good.*

"Let me fuck you, Sophie," he pleads.

"And if I say no?" I gasp, trying not to writhe under the erotic onslaught of his fingers.

"Then you die without experiencing this." He pinches my clit.

I cry out. I'm so close to coming.

He nibbles a trail of fire down my neck. "I'll make it good for you. So good."

My knees weaken and my core throbs with need. I glance down at the engagement ring. It shimmers from around my neck as if it senses my indecision.

Just say no, Sophie. It's not that hard. I know Logan would stay true to me until the end.

But I'm not Logan and I want to experience passion

before I die. My fingers are shaky and it takes two tries for me to unclasp the necklace. I toss it on the desk where it ironically lands smack on top of Logan's letter. I shut my eyes. *Out of sight out of mind, right?*

Taking a deep breath, I whisper the one word that will change everything. "Yes."

DID YOU ENJOY THIS PREVIEW OF CLAIMING THE BRIDE?

You can find it available for free here: https://BookHip.com/QCGGKF

Please don't forget to leave a review if you enjoyed this work!

www.ingramcontent.com/pod-product-compliance
Lightning Source LLC
Chambersburg PA
CBHW050519190726
48284CB00003B/862